The

Boy at the

Top of the

Mountain

The
Boy at the
Top of the
Mountain

JOHN BOYNE

SQUARE
FISH

Henry Holt and Company

NEW YORK

🏴
SQUARE
FISH

An imprint of Macmillan Publishing Group, LLC
175 Fifth Avenue
New York, NY 10010
mackids.com

Library of Congress Cataloging-in-Publication Data
Boyne, John, 1971–
The boy at the top of the mountain / John Boyne.
pages   cm
Summary: "A young orphan ends up living in Hitler's home
during WWII"—Provided by publisher.
ISBN 978-1-250-11505-8 (paperback)   ISBN 978-1-62779-542-5 (ebook)
[1. Orphans—Fiction.   2. World War, 1939–1945—Fiction.
3. Berghof (Obersalzberg, Germany)—Fiction.
4. Hitler, Adolf, 1889–1945—Fiction.]   I. Title.
PZ7.B69677Bo 2016   [Fic]—dc23   2015014263

First published in hardcover in 2015 by Doubleday Children's
First published in the United States by Henry Holt and Company in 2016
First Square Fish edition: 2017
Square Fish logo designed by Filomena Tuosto

1 3 5 7 9 10 8 6 4 2

LEXILE: 970L

For my nephews, Martin and Kevin

The Boy at the Top of the Mountain

Part

1

1936

Chapter

1

Three Red Spots on a Handkerchief

Although Pierrot Fischer's father didn't die in the Great War, his mother, Émilie, always maintained it was the war that killed him.

Pierrot wasn't the only seven-year-old in Paris who lived with just one parent. The boy who sat in front of him at school hadn't laid eyes on his mother in the four years since she'd run off with an encyclopedia salesman, while the classroom bully, who called Pierrot "Le Petit" because he was so small, had a room above his grandparents' tobacco shop on the Avenue de la Motte-Picquet, where he spent most of his time dropping water balloons from the upstairs window onto the heads of passersby below and then insisting that it had nothing to do with him.

And in an apartment on the ground floor of his own building on the nearby Avenue Charles-Floquet, Pierrot's best friend, Anshel Bronstein, lived alone with his mother, Madame Bronstein, his father having drowned two years earlier during an unsuccessful attempt to swim the English Channel.

Having been born only weeks apart, Pierrot and Anshel had grown up practically as brothers, one mother taking care of both babies when the other needed a nap. But unlike a lot of brothers, they never argued. Anshel had been born deaf, so the boys had developed a sign language early on, communicating easily and expressing through nimble fingers everything they needed to say. They even created special symbols for each other to use instead of their names. Anshel gave Pierrot the sign of the dog, as he considered his friend to be both kind and loyal, while Pierrot adopted the sign of the fox for Anshel, who everyone said was the smartest boy in their class.

They spent most of their time together, kicking a soccer ball around in the Champ de Mars and reading the same books. So close was their friendship that Pierrot was the only person Anshel allowed to read the stories he wrote in his bedroom at night. Not even Madame Bronstein knew that her son wanted to be a writer.

This one's good, Pierrot would sign, his fingers fluttering in the air as he handed back a bundle of pages. *I liked the bit about the horse and the part where the gold is discovered hidden in the coffin. This one's not so good,* he

4

would continue, handing back a second sheaf. *But that's because your handwriting is so terrible that I wasn't able to read some parts. . . . And this one*, he would add, waving a third pile in the air as if he were at a parade. *This one doesn't make any sense at all. I'd throw this one away if I were you.*

It's experimental, signed Anshel, who didn't mind criticism but could sometimes be a little defensive about the stories his friend enjoyed the least.

No, signed Pierrot, shaking his head. *It just doesn't make any sense. You should never let anyone read this one. They'll think you've lost your marbles.*

Pierrot, too, liked the idea of writing stories, but he could never sit still long enough to put the words down on the page. Instead, he sat on a chair opposite his friend and just started signing, making things up or describing some escapade at school, and Anshel would watch carefully before transcribing them for him later.

"So did I write this?" Pierrot would ask when he was finally given the pages and read through them.

"No, I wrote it," Anshel replied, shaking his head. "But it's your story."

Émilie, Pierrot's mother, rarely talked about his father anymore, although the boy still thought of him constantly. Wilhelm Fischer had lived with his wife and son until three years earlier, but he left Paris in the summer of 1933, a few months after his son's fourth birthday. Pierrot remembered his father as a tall man who would mimic the sounds of a horse as he carried the boy on his broad shoulders through the streets, breaking into an occasional gallop that always made Pierrot scream with delight. He taught his son German, to remind him of his ancestry, and did his best to help him learn simple songs on the piano, although Pierrot knew he would never be as accomplished as his father. Papa played folk songs that brought tears to the eyes of visitors, particularly when he sang along in that soft but powerful voice that spoke of memory and regret. If his musical skills were not great, Pierrot made up for this with his skill at languages; he could flit between speaking German to his father and French to his mother with no difficulty whatsoever. His party trick was singing "*La Marseillaise*" in German and then "*Das Deutschlandlied*" in French, a skill that sometimes made dinner guests uncomfortable.

"I don't want you doing that anymore, Pierrot," Maman told him one evening after his performance had caused a mild disagreement with some neighbors. "Learn something else if you want to show off. Juggling. Magic tricks. Standing on your head. Anything that doesn't involve singing in German."

"What's wrong with German?" asked Pierrot.

"Yes, Émilie," said Papa from the armchair in the corner, where he had spent the evening drinking too much wine, something that always left him brooding over the bad experiences that haunted him. "What's wrong with German?"

"Haven't you had enough, Wilhelm?" she asked, her hands pressed firmly to her hips as she turned to look at him.

"Enough of what? Enough of your friends insulting my country?"

"They weren't insulting it," she said. "They just find it difficult to forget the war, that's all. Particularly those who lost loved ones in the trenches."

"And yet they don't mind coming into my home, eating my food, and drinking my wine."

Papa waited until Maman had returned to the kitchen before summoning Pierrot and placing an arm around his waist. "Someday we will take back what's ours," he said, looking the boy directly in the eye. "And when we do, remember whose side you're on. You may have been born in France and you may live in Paris, but you're German through and through, just like me. Don't forget that, Pierrot."

Sometimes Papa woke in the middle of the night, his screams echoing through the dark and empty hallways of their apartment, and Pierrot's dog, D'Artagnan, would leap in fright from his basket, jump onto his bed, and scramble under the sheets next to his master, trembling. The boy would pull the blanket up to his chin, listening through the thin walls as Maman tried to calm Papa down, whispering in a low voice that he was fine, that he was at home with his family, that it had been nothing but a bad dream.

"But it wasn't a dream," he heard his father say once, his voice trembling with distress. "It was worse than that. It was a memory."

Occasionally Pierrot would wake in need of a quick trip to the bathroom and find his father seated at the kitchen table, his head slumped on the wooden surface, muttering to himself as an empty bottle lay on its side next to him. Whenever this happened, the boy would run downstairs in his bare feet and throw the bottle in the courtyard trash container so his mother wouldn't discover it the next morning. And usually, when he came back upstairs, Papa had roused himself and somehow found his way back to bed.

Neither father nor son ever talked about any of these things the next day.

Once, however, as Pierrot went outside on one of these late-night missions, he slipped on the wet staircase and tumbled to the floor—not badly enough to hurt himself but enough to smash the bottle he was holding. As he stood up a piece of glass embedded itself in the underside of his left foot. Grimacing, he pulled it out, but as it emerged, a thick stream of blood began to seep quickly through the torn skin; when he hobbled back into the apartment in search of a bandage, Papa woke and saw what he had been responsible for. After disinfecting the wound and ensuring that it was tightly wrapped, he sat the boy down and apologized for his drinking. Wiping away tears, he told Pierrot how much he loved him and promised that he would never do anything to put him in harm's way again.

"I love you, too, Papa," said Pierrot. "But I love most when you're carrying me on your shoulders and pretending to be a horse. I don't like it when you sit in the armchair and won't talk to me or Maman."

"I don't like those moments, either," said Papa quietly. "But sometimes it's as if a dark cloud has settled over me and I can't get it to move on. That's why I drink. It helps me forget."

"Forget what?"

"The war. The things I saw." He closed his eyes as he whispered, "The things I did."

Pierrot swallowed, almost afraid of asking the question. "What did you do?"

Papa offered him a sad smile. "Whatever I did, I did for my country," he said. "You can understand that, can't you?"

"Yes, Papa," said Pierrot, who wasn't sure what his father meant but thought it sounded valiant nevertheless. "I'd be a soldier, too, if it would make you proud of me."

Papa looked at his son and placed a hand on his shoulders. "Just make sure you pick the right side," he said.

For several weeks after this he stopped drinking. And then, just as abruptly as he had given up, that dark cloud he had spoken of returned, and he started again.

Papa worked as a waiter in a local restaurant, disappearing every morning around ten o'clock and returning at three before leaving again at six for the dinner service. On one occasion he came home in a bad mood and said that someone named Papa Joffre had been in the restaurant for lunch, seated at one of his tables; he had refused to serve him until his employer, Monsieur Abrahams, said that if he didn't, he could go home and never return.

"Who's Papa Joffre?" asked Pierrot, having never heard the name before.

"He was a great general in the war," said Maman, lifting a pile of clothes out of a basket and placing it next to her ironing board. "A hero to our people."

"To *your* people," said Papa.

"Remember that you married a Frenchwoman," said Maman, turning to him angrily.

"Because I loved her," replied Papa. "Pierrot, did I ever tell you about when I saw your mother for the first time? It was a couple of years after the Great War ended. I had arranged to meet my sister, Beatrix, during her lunch break, and when I got to the department store where she worked, she was talking to one of the new assistants, a shy creature who had only started that week. I took one look at her and knew immediately that this was the girl I was going to marry."

Pierrot smiled; he loved it when his father told stories like this.

"I opened my mouth to speak but couldn't find any words. It was as if my brain had just gone to sleep. And so I just stood there, staring, saying nothing."

"I thought there was something wrong with him," said Maman, smiling, too, at the memory.

"Beatrix had to shake me by the shoulders," said Papa, laughing at his own foolishness.

"If it wasn't for her, I would never have agreed to go out with you," added Maman. "She told me that I should take a chance. That you were not as odd as you seemed."

"Why don't we ever see Aunt Beatrix?" asked Pierrot, for he had heard her name on a few occasions over the years but had never met her. She never came to visit and never wrote any letters.

"Because we don't," said Papa, the smile leaving his face now as his expression changed.

"But why not?"

"Leave it, Pierrot," he said.

"Yes, leave it, Pierrot," repeated Maman, her face

clouding over now, too. "Because that's what we do in this house. We push away the people we love, we don't talk about things that matter, and we don't allow anyone to help us."

And just like that, a happy conversation was spoiled.

"He eats like a pig," said Papa a few minutes later, crouching down and looking Pierrot in the eye, curling his fingers into claws. "Papa Joffre, I mean. Like a rat chewing his way along a cob of corn."

Week after week, Papa complained about how low his wages were, how Monsieur and Madame Abrahams spoke down to him, and how the Parisians had grown increasingly stingy with their tips. "This is why we never have any money," he grumbled. "They're all so tight-fisted. Especially the Jews—they're the worst. And they come in all the time because they say that Madame Abrahams makes the best gefilte fish and latkes in all of Western Europe."

"Anshel is Jewish," said Pierrot quietly. He had often seen his friend leaving for temple with his mother.

"Anshel is one of the good ones," muttered Papa. "They say every barrel of good apples contains a single rotten one. Well, that works the other way around, too."

"We never have any money," said Maman, interrupting him, "because you spend most of what you earn on wine. And you shouldn't speak about our neighbors like that. Remember how—"

"You think I bought this?" he asked, picking up a bottle and turning it around to show her the label—the same house wine that the restaurant used. "Your mother can be very naive sometimes," he added in German to Pierrot.

Despite everything, Pierrot loved spending time with his father. Once a month Papa would take him to the Tuileries Garden, where he would name the different trees and plants that lined the walkways, explaining how each one changed as season followed season. His own parents, he told him, had been avid horticulturalists and had loved anything to do with the land. "But they lost it all, of course," he added. "Their farm was taken from them. All their hard work destroyed. They never recovered."

On the way home he bought ice creams from a street seller, and when Pierrot's fell to the ground, his father gave him his instead.

These were the things that he tried to remember whenever there was trouble at home. Only a few weeks later an argument broke out in their front parlor when some neighbors—not the same as those who had objected to Pierrot's singing *"La Marseillaise"* in German—began discussing politics. Voices were raised, old grievances aired, and when they left, his parents got into a terrible fight.

"If you'd only stop drinking," Maman cried. "Alcohol makes you say the most terrible things. Can't you see how much you upset people?"

"I drink to forget," shouted Papa. "You haven't seen the things I've seen. You don't have these images going around in your head day and night."

"But it's so long ago," she said, stepping closer to him and reaching across to take his arm. "Please, Wilhelm, I know how much it hurts you, but perhaps it's because you refuse to talk about it sensibly. Maybe if you shared your pain with me—"

Émilie never got to finish that sentence, for at that moment Wilhelm did a very bad thing, a thing he had done for the first time a few months earlier, swearing that he would never do again, although he had broken this promise several times since then. As upset as she was, Pierrot's mother always found some way to excuse his behavior, particularly when she found her son crying in his bedroom at the frightening scenes he had witnessed.

"You mustn't blame him," she said.

"But he hurts you," said Pierrot, looking up with tears in his eyes. On the bed, D'Artagnan glanced from one to the other before jumping down and nuzzling his nose into his master's side. The little dog always knew when Pierrot was upset.

"He's ill," replied Émilie, holding a hand to her face. "And when someone we love is ill, it's our job to help them get better. If they will let us. But if they won't . . ." She took a deep breath before speaking again. "Pierrot," she said, "how would you feel if we were to move away?"

"All of us?"

She shook her head. "No," she said. "Just you and me."

"And what about Papa?"

Maman sighed, and Pierrot could see the tears forming in her eyes. "All I know," she said, "is that things can't go on as they are."

The last time Pierrot saw his father was on a warm May evening, shortly after his fourth birthday, when once again the kitchen was littered with empty bottles and Papa began shouting and banging the sides of his head with his hands, complaining that they were in there, they were all in there, they were coming to get their revenge on him—phrases that made no sense to Pierrot. Papa reached over to the cupboard and threw handfuls of plates, bowls, and cups onto the floor, smashing them into hundreds of pieces. Maman held her arms out to him, pleading with him in an attempt to calm his temper,

but he lashed out, punching her in the face and screaming words that were so terrible that Pierrot covered his
ears and ran into his bedroom with D'Artagnan, and
they hid in the wardrobe together. Pierrot was shaking
and trying not to cry as the little dog, who hated any
kind of disturbance, whimpered and curled himself into
the boy's body.

Pierrot didn't leave the wardrobe for hours, until
everything had grown quiet again, and when he did, his
father had vanished and his mother was lying on the
floor, motionless, her face bloody and bruised. D'Artagnan
walked over cautiously, bowing his head and licking
her ear repeatedly in an attempt to wake her, but Pierrot
simply stared in disbelief. Summoning all his courage,
he ran downstairs to Anshel's apartment, where he
pointed toward the staircase, unable to utter a word of
explanation. Madame Bronstein, who must have heard
the earlier commotion through her ceiling but was too
frightened to intervene, ran upstairs, taking the steps
two or three at a time. Meanwhile, Pierrot looked across
at his friend, one boy unable to speak, the other unable
to hear; noticing a pile of pages on the table behind him,
he walked over, sat down, and began to read Anshel's
latest story. Somehow he found that losing himself in a
world that wasn't his own was a welcome escape.

For several weeks there was no word from Papa, and
Pierrot both longed for and dreaded his return, and then

one morning word came to them that Wilhelm had died when he fell beneath a train that was making its way from Munich to Penzberg, the same town where he was born and had spent his childhood. When he heard the news, Pierrot went to his room, locked the door, looked at the dog, who was snoozing on the bed, and spoke very calmly.

"Papa is looking down at us now, D'Artagnan," he said. "And one day I am going to make him proud of me."

Afterward, Monsieur and Madame Abrahams offered Émilie work as a waitress, which Madame Bronstein said was in poor taste, as they were simply offering her the job that her dead husband had had before her. But Maman, who knew that they needed the money, accepted gratefully.

The restaurant was halfway between Pierrot's school and home, and he would read and draw in the small room downstairs every afternoon while the staff wandered in and out, taking their breaks, chatting about the customers, and generally fussing over him. Madame Abrahams always brought him down a plate of whatever that day's special was, with a bowl of ice cream to follow.

Pierrot spent three years, from the ages of four to seven, sitting in that room every afternoon while Maman served customers upstairs, and although he never spoke of him, he thought of his father every day, picturing him standing there, changing into his uniform in the morning, counting his tips at the end of the day.

Years later, when Pierrot looked back on his childhood, he experienced complicated emotions. Although he was very sad about his father, he had plenty of friends and enjoyed school, and he and Maman lived happily together. Paris was flourishing, and the streets were always buzzing with people and energy.

But in 1936, on Émilie's birthday, what should have been a happy day took a turn toward tragedy. In the evening Madame Bronstein and Anshel had come upstairs with a small cake to celebrate, and Pierrot and his friend were munching on a second slice when, quite unexpectedly, Maman began to cough. At first, Pierrot thought that a piece of cake must have gone down the wrong way, but the coughing continued much longer than seemed normal, and only when Madame Bronstein gave her a glass of water to drink did it come to an end. When she recovered, however, her eyes appeared bloodshot and she pressed a hand to her chest as if she was in pain.

"I'm fine," she said as her breathing returned to normal. "I must be getting a chill, that's all."

"But, my dear . . . ," said Madame Bronstein, her face growing pale as she pointed toward the handkerchief that Émilie held in her hands. Pierrot glanced across, and his mouth fell open when he saw three small spots of blood in the center of the linen. Maman stared at them, too, for a few moments before crumpling it up and tucking it away inside her pocket. Then, placing both hands carefully on the arms of her chair, she rose, smoothed down her dress, and attempted to smile.

"Émilie, are you quite all right?" asked Madame Bronstein, standing up, and Pierrot's mother nodded quickly.

"It's nothing," she said. "Probably just a little throat infection, although I am a little tired. Perhaps I should get some sleep. You were so thoughtful to bring the cake, but if you and Anshel don't mind . . . ?"

"Of course, of course," replied Madame Bronstein, tapping her son on the shoulder and making her way toward the door with more urgency than Pierrot had ever seen before. "If you need anything, just stamp on the floor a few times and I'll be up in a flash."

Maman didn't cough any more that night, or for several days afterward, but then, while she was waiting on some customers in the restaurant, she seemed to lose control of herself entirely and was brought downstairs to where Pierrot was playing chess with one of the waiters. This time, her face was gray and her handkerchief was not spotted with blood but covered in it. Perspiration ran down her face, and when Dr. Chibaud arrived, he took one look at her and called for an ambulance. Within an hour she was lying in a bed in the Hôtel-Dieu hospital as the doctors examined her and whispered among themselves, their voices low and worried.

Pierrot spent that night in the Bronsteins' apartment, top-to-tail in the bed with Anshel, while D'Artagnan snored on the floor. He felt very frightened, of course, and would have liked to talk to his friend about what was happening, but as good as his sign language was, it was no use to him in the dark.

He visited Maman every day for a week, and each day she seemed to be struggling for breath more and more. He was the only one with her on that Sunday afternoon when her breathing began to slow down entirely and her fingers fell loose around his own; then her head slipped to one side of the pillow, her eyes still open, and he knew that she was gone.

Pierrot sat very still for a few minutes before quietly pulling the curtain around the bed and returning to the chair next to his mother, holding her hand and refusing to let go. Finally an elderly nurse arrived, saw what had happened, and told him that she needed to move Émilie to a different place, where her body could be prepared for the undertaker. At these words, Pierrot burst into tears that he felt might never end and clung to his mother's body while the nurse tried to console him. It took a long time for him to calm down, and when he did, his entire body felt broken on the inside. He had never known pain like this before.

"I want her to have this," he said, retrieving a photograph of his father from his pocket and placing it next to her on the bed.

The nurse nodded and promised that she would make sure the picture remained with Maman.

"Don't you have any family I can call for you?" she asked.

"No," said Pierrot, shaking his head, unable to look her in the eye in case he saw either pity or lack of interest there. "No, there's no one. It's just me. I'm all alone now."

Chapter

2

The Medal in the Cabinet

Born only a year apart, neither Simone nor Adèle Durand had ever married. They seemed content in each other's company, even though the sisters were not at all alike.

Simone, the elder of the two, was surprisingly tall, towering over most men. A very beautiful woman with dark skin and deep brown eyes, she had an artistic soul and liked nothing more than to sit at the piano for hours on end, lost in her music. Adèle, on the other hand, was rather short, with a fat bottom and a sallow complexion, and waddled around like a duck, a species of bird she rather resembled. She was constantly active and easily the more sociable of the pair, but didn't have a musical note in her head.

The sisters grew up in a large mansion about eighty miles to the south of Paris in the city of Orléans, where, five hundred years before, Joan of Arc had famously lifted the city's siege. When they were very young, they believed that they belonged to the largest family in France, for there were almost fifty other children, aged from just a few weeks old to seventeen, living in the dormitories on the third, fourth, and fifth floors of their house. Some were friendly, some were angry, some were shy, and some were bullies, but they all had one thing in common: They were orphans. Their voices and footsteps were audible from the family quarters on the first floor below as they talked before bedtime or ran around in the morning, shrieking as their bare feet skittered along the cold marble floors. But although Simone and Adèle shared a home with them, they felt separated from the other children in a way that they did not fully understand until they were older.

Monsieur and Madame Durand, the girls' parents, had set up the orphanage after they married and ran it until their deaths, with some very strict policies about who could be admitted and who could not. When they were gone, the sisters took over, devoting themselves entirely to the care of children who had been left on their own in the world, and changing some of those policies in important ways.

"Every child who is alone will be welcome," they declared. "Color, race, or creed mean nothing to us."

Simone and Adèle were exceptionally close, walking around the grounds together every day as they examined the flower beds and gave instructions to the gardener. Apart from their physical appearance, the thing that truly distinguished the sisters was that Adèle could scarcely seem to stop talking from the moment she woke in the morning until the minute she fell asleep at night, while Simone rarely spoke at all. When she did, it was in brief sentences, as if each breath might cost her energy that she could scarcely afford to waste.

Pierrot met the Durand sisters almost a month after his mother's death, when he boarded a train at the Gare d'Austerlitz, wearing his best clothes and a brand-new scarf that Madame Bronstein had purchased for him in the Galeries Lafayette as a parting gift the afternoon before. She, Anshel, and D'Artagnan had come to the station to see him off, and with every step he took, Pierrot felt his heart sinking a little deeper inside his chest. He was frightened and lonely, filled with grief for Maman, and wished that he and his dog could move in with his best friend. In fact, he *had* stayed with Anshel in the weeks after the funeral, and had watched as Madame Bronstein and her son went to temple together on the Sabbath, even asking whether he could go with them; but she had said that wasn't a good idea right now and that he should take D'Artagnan out for a walk in the Champ de Mars instead. As the days went on, Madame Bronstein returned one afternoon with one of her friends, and he overheard the visitor saying that she had a cousin who had adopted a Gentile child and he'd quickly become part of the family.

"The problem isn't that he's a Gentile, Ruth," said Madame Bronstein. "The problem is that I simply don't have enough money to keep him. I don't have much; that's the truth of it. Levi left me with very little. Oh, I put on a good show, or try to, but it's not easy for a widow on her own. And what I have I need for Anshel."

"You have to look after your own first, of course you do," said the lady. "But isn't there anyone who could—"

"I've tried. Believe me, I've spoken to everyone I can think of. I don't suppose you'd—"

"No, I'm sorry. Times are hard; you've said so yourself. And besides, life isn't getting any easier for Jews in Paris, is it? The boy might be better off in a family more like his own."

"Perhaps you're right. I'm sorry. I shouldn't even have asked."

"Of course you should. You're doing your best for the boy. That's who you are. That's who *we* are. But when it's not possible, it's not possible. So when will you tell him?"

"Tonight, I think. It's not going to be easy."

Pierrot went back to Anshel's room and puzzled over this conversation before looking up the word *Gentile* in a dictionary and wondering what that had to do with anything anyway. He sat there for a long time, tossing Anshel's yarmulke, which hung from the back of a chair, between his hands; later, when Madame Bronstein came in to speak to him, he was wearing it on his head.

"Take that off," she snapped, reaching forward and grabbing it before putting it back where he had found it. It was the first time in his life she'd ever spoken to him harshly. "You don't play with something like this. It's not a toy; it's sacred."

Pierrot said nothing, but he felt a mixture of embarrassment and distress. He wasn't allowed to go to temple, he wasn't allowed to wear his best friend's cap; it was obvious to him that he wasn't wanted there. And when she told him where he was being sent, there was simply no doubt about it.

"I'm so sorry, Pierrot," said Madame Bronstein after she'd finished explaining things to him. "But I have heard only good things about this orphanage. I'm sure you'll be happy there. And perhaps a wonderful family will adopt you soon."

"But what about D'Artagnan?" asked Pierrot, looking down at the little dog, who was snoozing on the floor.

"We can look after him," said Madame Bronstein. "He likes bones, doesn't he?"

"He loves bones."

"Well, they're free, thanks to Monsieur Abrahams. He said he'd let me have a few every day for nothing because he and his wife cared for your mother so deeply."

Pierrot said nothing; he was sure that if things were

26

different, Maman would have taken Anshel in. Despite what Madame Bronstein had said, it must have had something to do with the fact that he was a Gentile. For now, he was simply frightened by the idea of being alone in the world and felt sad that Anshel and D'Artagnan would have each other while he would have no one at all.

I hope I don't forget how to do this, signed Pierrot as he waited with his friend on the station concourse that morning while Madame Bronstein purchased his one-way ticket.

You just said that you hope you won't become an eagle, signed Anshel, laughing and showing his friend the signs that he should have made.

See? signed Pierrot, wishing that he could throw all the different shapes in the air and let them fall back into his fingers in the proper order. *I'm already forgetting*.

No, you're not. You're still learning, that's all.

You're so much better at it than I am.

Anshel smiled. *I have to be.*

Pierrot turned as he heard the sound of the steam escaping from the valves of the train's smoke box and the harsh blast of the conductor's whistle, a furious call-to-platform that made his stomach turn over in anxiety. There was a part of him, of course, that was a little excited about this part of his journey, for he'd never been on a train before, but he just wished that the trip would never come to an end, because he was scared of what might be waiting for him at the other end.

We can write to each other, Anshel, signed Pierrot. *We must never lose touch.*

Every week.

Pierrot made the sign of the fox, Anshel made the sign of the dog, and they held the two symbols in the air to represent their eternal friendship. They wanted to give each other a hug, but there were so many people around that they felt a little embarrassed and so shook hands instead as Pierrot took his leave.

"Good-bye, Pierrot," said Madame Bronstein, leaning down to give him a kiss, and the noise of the train was so loud now, and the bustle of the crowds so overwhelming, that it was almost impossible to hear her.

"It's because I'm not a Jew, isn't it?" said Pierrot, looking directly at her. "You don't like Gentiles, and you don't want one to live with you."

"What?" she asked, standing up straight and looking shocked. "Pierrot, whatever gave you that idea? That was the last thing on my mind! Anyway, you're a smart boy. Surely you can see how attitudes toward Jews are changing here—the names we get called, the resentment people seem to feel toward us."

"But if I was a Jew, you'd find a way to keep me with you, I know you would."

28

"You're wrong, Pierrot. I'm just thinking about your safety and—"

"All aboard!" cried the conductor loudly. "Last call! All aboard!"

"Good-bye, Anshel," Pierrot said, turning away from her and making his way up the step into the train car.

"Pierrot!" cried Madame Bronstein. "Come back please! Let me explain—you have it all wrong!"

But he didn't turn around. His time in Paris was over; he knew that now. He closed the door behind him, took a deep breath, and stepped forward to begin his new life.

Within an hour and a half, the conductor was tapping Pierrot on the shoulder and pointing toward the church steeples that were just coming into sight. "Now then," he said, pointing to the piece of paper that Madame Bronstein had pinned to his lapel and on which she had written his name—*PIERROT FISCHER*—and his destination—*ORLÉANS*—in big black letters. "This is your stop."

Pierrot swallowed hard, took his small suitcase out from under the seat, and made his way to the door just as the train pulled in. As he stepped onto the platform, he waited for the steam from the engines to clear to see whether anyone was waiting for him. A momentary panic left him wondering what he would do if no one showed up. Who would take care of him? He was only seven years old, after all, and he had no money for a ticket back to Paris. How would he eat? Where would he sleep? What would become of him?

He felt someone tap him on the shoulder, and when he turned around, a red-faced man reached down to rip the note from his collar, holding it close to his eyes before crumpling it up and throwing it away.

"You're with me," he said, making his way toward a horse and cart while Pierrot gazed at him, rooted to the spot. "Get a move on," he added, turning around and staring at him. "My time's precious even if yours isn't."

"Who are you?" asked Pierrot, refusing to follow him in case he was simply being taken into servitude by some farmer who needed extra help with his harvest. Anshel had once written a story about just such a boy, and it had ended badly for everyone involved.

"Who am I?" asked the man, laughing at the audacity of the boy's question. "I'm the fellow who's going to tan your hide if you don't hop to it."

Pierrot's eyes opened wide. He hadn't been in Orléans for more than a couple of minutes and he was already being threatened with violence. He shook his head defiantly and sat down on his suitcase. "I'm sorry," he said. "I'm not supposed to go anywhere with strangers."

"Don't worry, we won't be strangers for long," said

the man, his face softening a little as he smiled. He was about fifty years old and looked a little like Monsieur Abrahams from the restaurant, except for the fact that he hadn't shaved in a few days and was wearing scruffy old clothes that didn't match very well. "You're Pierrot Fischer, aren't you? It says so on your lapel anyway. The Durand sisters sent me to get you. My name's Houper. I do a few odd jobs for them now and then. And sometimes I come to collect the orphans from the train station. The ones who travel on their own, that is."

"Oh," said Pierrot, standing up now. "I thought they would come to fetch me themselves."

"And leave all those little monsters with the run of the place? Not likely. The place would be in ruins by the time they got back." The man stepped forward, and his tone changed as he lifted Pierrot's suitcase. "Look, there's nothing to be frightened of," he said. "It's a good place. They're very kind, the pair of them. So what do you think—will you come with me?"

Pierrot glanced around. The train had moved on now, and from where he was standing, there was nothing to be seen for miles around except fields. He knew that he had no choice.

"All right," he said.

Within the hour, Pierrot found himself seated in a neat and orderly office with two enormous windows looking over a well-tended garden. The Durand sisters looked him up and down as if he were something they were considering buying at a fair.

"How old are you?" asked Simone, holding up a pair of spectacles to examine him before letting them fall and hang loose around her neck.

"I'm seven," said Pierrot.

"You can't be seven. You're far too small."

"I've always been small," replied Pierrot. "But I plan on getting bigger one day."

"Do you indeed," said Simone doubtfully.

"Such a lovely age, seven," said Adèle, clapping her hands together and smiling. "Children are always so happy then, and so full of wonder about the world."

"My dear," interrupted Simone, laying a hand on her sister's arm. "The boy's mother has just died. I doubt that he is feeling particularly jovial."

"Oh, of course, of course," said Adèle, her face growing serious now. "You must still be grieving. It's a terrible thing, the loss of a loved one. A terrible thing. My sister and I understand that only too well. I only meant that boys of your age are rather charming, I think. You only start to turn nasty when you hit thirteen or fourteen. Not that you will go that way, I'm sure. I daresay you will be one of the good ones."

"My dear," repeated Simone quietly.

"I'm sorry," replied Adèle. "I'm prattling on, amn't I? Let me say this, then." She cleared her throat as if she were about to address a room full of unruly factory workers. "We are very happy to have you here with us, Pierrot. I have no doubt that you will be a tremendous asset to what we like to think of as our little family here at the orphanage. And my goodness, aren't you a handsome little fellow! You have the most extraordinary blue eyes. I used to own a spaniel with eyes just like yours. Not that I'm comparing you to a dog, of course. That would be terribly rude. I only meant that you put me in mind of him, that's all. Simone, don't Pierrot's eyes remind you of Casper's?"

Simone raised an eyebrow and glanced at the boy for a moment before shaking her head. "No," she said.

"Oh, but they do, they really do!" declared Adèle with so much delight that Pierrot began to wonder whether she thought her dead dog had come back to life in human form. "Now, first things first." And here her expression turned quite serious. "We were both so sorry to hear about what happened with your dear mother. So young and such a wonderful provider, from what we've been told. And after all she'd been through in her life, too. It seems terribly cruel that someone with so much to live for should be taken away from you just when you need her the most. And I daresay she loved you very much. Don't you agree, Simone? Don't you think that Madame Fischer must have loved Pierrot very much?"

Simone looked up from a ledger into which she was writing details of Pierrot's height and physical condition.

"I imagine that most mothers love their sons," she said. "It's hardly worth commenting upon."

"And your father," continued Adèle. "He passed away a few years ago, too, isn't that right?"

"Yes," said Pierrot.

"And you have no other family?"

"No. Well, my father had a sister, I think, but I've never met her. She never came to visit. She probably doesn't even know that I'm alive or that my parents are dead. I don't have her address."

"Oh, what a shame!"

"How long will I have to stay here?" Pierrot asked, his attention drawn to the many pictures and drawings on display. On the desk he noticed a photograph of a man and woman seated on two chairs with a large gap between them, such serious expressions on their faces that he wondered whether they had been captured in the middle of an argument; he knew by looking at them that they were the sisters' parents. Another photograph, placed on the opposite corner of the desk, revealed two little girls holding hands with a slightly younger boy who was standing between them. On the wall was a third photograph, a portrait of a young man with a pencil mustache wearing a French army uniform. The picture was taken in profile, so from where it hung, the young man was staring out the window into the gardens beyond with a rather wistful expression on his face.

"Many of our orphans are placed with good families within a month or two of their arrival," said Adèle, sitting down on the couch and indicating that Pierrot should take a seat next to her. "There are so many wonderful men and women who would like to start a family but have not been blessed with children of their own; others simply want to bring an extra brother or sister into their home out of kindness and charity. You must never underestimate how kind people can be, Pierrot."

"Or how cruel," muttered Simone from behind her desk. Pierrot glanced across at her in surprise, but she didn't look up.

"We've had some children who were with us for only a few days or weeks," continued Adèle, ignoring her sister's remark. "And some who were here a little longer, of course. But once, a little boy of your age was brought to us in the morning and he was gone again by lunchtime. We barely had a chance to get to know him at all, did we, Simone?"

"No," said Simone.

"What was his name?"

"I can't remember."

"Well, it doesn't matter," said Adèle. "The point is that you can't predict when someone will find a family. Something like that might happen to you, Pierrot."

"It's almost five o'clock," he replied. "The day's almost over."

35

"I only meant—"

"And how many never get adopted?" he asked.

"Hmm? What's that?"

"How many children never get adopted?" he repeated. "How many live here until they're grown up?"

"Ah," said Adèle, her smile fading a little. "Well, it's difficult to put a number on that, of course. It happens occasionally, of course it does, but I very much doubt that it will happen with you. Why, any family would be delighted to have you! But let's not worry about that for now. However long or short your stay may be, we'll try to make it as enjoyable as possible. For now the important thing is that you get settled in, meet your new friends, and start to feel at home. You may have heard some bad stories about the types of things that go on in orphanages, Pierrot, because there are an awful lot of people who tell terrible stories—and then there was that horrible Englishman, Mr. Dickens, who gave us all a bad name with his novels—but you can rest assured that nothing untoward goes on in our establishment. We run a happy house for all our boys and girls, and if there's ever a moment when you feel frightened or alone, you simply have to come looking for either Simone or me, and we will be happy to help you. Won't we, Simone?"

"Adèle is usually quite easy to find," replied the older sister.

"Where will I sleep?" asked Pierrot. "Do I get my own room?"

"Oh no," said Adèle. "Even Simone and I don't have our own rooms. This isn't the Palace of Versailles, you know! No, we have dormitories here. Separate dormitories for boys and girls, of course, so you don't need to worry about that. They each have ten beds in them, although the room you're going into is a little quiet at the moment, so you'll only be the seventh boy in there. You can take your pick of the empty beds. All we ask is that when you choose one, you stick with it. It makes everything easier on wash day. You'll take a bath every Wednesday night, although"—and here she leaned forward and sniffed the air a little—"it might be for the best if you take one this evening, too, just to wash the dust of Paris and the filth of the train away. You're a little ripe, dear. We rise at six thirty, then there's breakfast, school, lunch, a little more school, then games, dinner, and bed. You'll love it here, Pierrot, I'm sure you will. And we will do our very best to find a wonderful family for you. That's the funny thing about this line of work, you see. We're so happy to see you arrive, but we're even happier to see you leave. Isn't that right, Simone?"

"Yes," agreed Simone.

Adèle stood up and invited Pierrot to follow her so she could show him around the orphanage, but as he walked toward the door, he noticed something sparkling inside a small glass cabinet and walked over to look at it. He pressed his face against the glass and squinted as he stared at a circle of bronze, with a figure at its center, hanging from a strip of red-and-white striped fabric. A separate bronze bar was clipped to the material, inscribed with the words *Engagé Volontaire*. At the base of the cabinet stood a small candle and another photograph, a smaller one, of the man with the pencil mustache, smiling and waving from a train as it pulled out of a station. He recognized the platform immediately, for it was the same one where he had disembarked from the Paris train earlier in the day.

"What's that?" asked Pierrot, pointing at the medal. "And who's he?"

"That has nothing to do with you," said Simone, standing up now, and Pierrot spun around, feeling a little nervous as he saw the serious expression on her face. "You are never to touch that or interfere with it in any way. Adèle, take him to his room. Now, please!"

Chapter

3

A Letter from a Friend and a Letter from a Stranger

Things were not quite as wonderful in the orphanage as Adèle Durand had suggested. The beds were hard and the sheets were thin. When the food was plentiful, it was usually tasteless, and when it was scarce, it was usually good.

Pierrot did his best to make friends, although it wasn't easy when the other children knew one another so well and were wary of allowing newcomers into their groups. There were a few who liked reading, but they wouldn't let Pierrot join their discussions because he hadn't read the same books as they had. There were others who had spent months creating a miniature village from wood they'd gathered in the nearby forest, but they shook their heads and said that since Pierrot didn't know the difference between a bevel and a block plane, they couldn't allow him to ruin something they'd worked so hard on. A group of boys who played soccer in the grounds every afternoon, naming themselves after their favorite players on the French national team— Courtois, Mattler, Delfour—*did* allow Pierrot to play with them, once, in goal, but after his side lost eleven– nil, they said he wasn't tall enough to jump for the high shots. All the other positions on the teams were taken.

"Sorry, Pierrot," they said, not sounding sorry at all.

The only person he spent much time with was a girl a year or two older, Josette, who had arrived at the orphanage three years earlier after her parents were killed in a train crash near Toulouse. She'd been adopted twice already, but on both occasions she'd been sent back like an unwanted parcel when the families declared her "too disruptive" for their households.

"The first couple was awful," she told Pierrot as they sat under a tree one morning, their toes sinking into the dew-dampened grass. "They refused to call me Josette. They said they'd always wanted a daughter named Marie-Louise. The second just wanted an unpaid servant. They had me cleaning floors and washing dishes from morning till night like Cinderella. So I caused mayhem until they let me leave. Anyway, I like Simone and Adèle," she added. "Maybe someday I'll allow myself to be adopted. But not just yet. I'm perfectly happy where I am."

The worst orphan of all was a boy named Hugo, who had lived there his entire life—eleven years—and was considered the most important but also the most intimidating child under the Durand sisters' care. He had long hair, down to his shoulders, and slept in the same dormitory as Pierrot, who'd made the mistake of choosing the bed next to him on his arrival. He snored so loudly that Pierrot sometimes had to bury himself deep under the sheets to block out the noise, and even took to putting ripped-up pieces of newspaper in his ears at night to see whether that might help. Simone and Adèle never put Hugo up for adoption, and when couples arrived to meet the children, he stayed in his room, never washing his face or putting on a clean shirt or smiling at the adults as the rest of the orphans did.

Hugo spent most of his time wandering the corridors in search of someone to bully. And Pierrot, who was small and thin, was the obvious target.

The bullying took several forms, none of which was particularly imaginative. Sometimes Hugo would wait until Pierrot was asleep before placing his left hand in a bowl of warm water—which would lead Pierrot to do something that he had generally stopped doing by the time he was three years old. Sometimes he would hold the back of Pierrot's seat when he was trying to sit down in class and force him to keep standing until the teacher scolded him. Sometimes he would hide his towel after his bath, leaving Pierrot to run red-faced back to the dormitory, where all the other boys would start laughing and pointing at him. And sometimes he relied on more traditional and time-proven methods—simply waiting for Pierrot to come around a corner, when he would jump on him, pull his hair, punch him in the stomach, and leave him with torn clothes and bruises.

"Who's doing this to you?" asked Adèle when she found him sitting on his own by the lake one afternoon, examining a cut on his arm. "If there's one thing I won't stand for, Pierrot, it's bullying."

"I can't tell you," said Pierrot, unable to lift his eyes from the ground. He didn't like the idea of being a snitch.

"But you must," she insisted. "Otherwise, there's nothing I can do to help you. Is it Laurent? He's been in trouble for this sort of thing before."

"No, it's not Laurent," said Pierrot, shaking his head.

"Sylvestre, then?" she asked. "That boy is always up to no good."

"No," said Pierrot. "It's not Sylvestre, either."

Adèle looked away and sighed deeply. "It's Hugo, isn't it?" she said after a long silence, and something in her tone made Pierrot realize that she had known it was Hugo all along but had hoped she might be wrong.

Pierrot said nothing, simply kicked a few pebbles with the tip of his right shoe and watched as they tumbled down the bank and disappeared beneath the surface of the water. "Can I go back to the dormitory?" he asked.

Adèle nodded, and as he walked across the gardens, he knew that her eyes were watching him all the way.

The following afternoon, Pierrot and Josette were taking a walk through the grounds in search of a family of frogs they'd encountered a few days earlier. He was telling her about the letter he'd received that morning from Anshel.

"What do you talk about in your letters?" asked Josette, rather intrigued by this idea, as she never received any mail.

"Well, he's looking after my dog, D'Artagnan," replied Pierrot. "So he tells me all about him. And he lets me know what's going on in the streets where I grew up. Apparently there was a riot nearby. I'm quite glad I missed that, though."

Josette had read about the riot herself a week earlier, in an article that declared that all Jews should be guillotined. But then more and more of the newspapers were carrying articles condemning the Jews and wishing that they would all just go away, and she read each one intently.

"And he sends me his stories," continued Pierrot, "because he wants to be a—"

Before he could finish his sentence, Hugo and his two pals, Gérard and Marc, appeared from behind a cluster of trees, carrying sticks.

"Well, look who it is," said Hugo, grinning as he rubbed the back of his hand against his nose to wipe away a long stream of something disgusting. "If it isn't the happy couple, Monsieur and Madame Fischer."

"Go away, Hugo," said Josette, trying to brush past him, but he jumped in front of her and shook his head, holding his two sticks in an X shape before him.

"This is my land," he said. "Anyone who walks through here must pay the forfeit."

Josette sighed deeply, as if she couldn't believe how annoying boys could be, and folded her arms, staring directly at him but refusing to give ground. Pierrot held back, wishing they had never come out here at all.

"All right, then," she said. "What's the forfeit?"

"Five francs," said Hugo.

"I'll owe it to you."

"Then I'll have to attach interest. Another franc for every day you go without paying."

"That's fine," said Josette. "Let me know when it hits a million, and I'll get in touch with my bank to make the transfer to your account."

"You think you're so clever, don't you?" Hugo said, rolling his eyes.

"Cleverer than you, that's for sure."

"As if."

"She is," said Pierrot, feeling that he'd better say something or end up looking like a coward.

Hugo turned to him with a half smile. "Standing up for your girlfriend, are you, Fischer?" he asked. "You're so in love with her, aren't you?" And then he made kissy noises in the air before turning and wrapping his arms around his own body, running his hands up and down his sides.

"Do you have any idea how ridiculous you look?" asked Josette, and Pierrot couldn't help but laugh, even though he knew it was not a good idea to provoke Hugo, whose face went even redder than usual at the insult.

"Don't get smart with me," he said, reaching out and poking her shoulder sharply with the tip of one of the sticks. "Just you remember who's in charge around here."

"Ha!" cried Josette. "You think you're in charge? As if anyone would ever let a filthy *Jew* be in charge of anything."

Hugo's face fell a little, and his brow furrowed in a mixture of confusion and disappointment. "Why would you say something like that?" he asked. "I was only playing."

"You never play, Hugo," she said, waving him away. "But you can't help it, can you? It's in your nature. What should I expect from a pig but a grunt?"

Pierrot frowned. So Hugo was a Jew, too? He wanted

to laugh at what Josette had said, but he remembered some of the things the boys in his class had said to Anshel and how badly they had upset his friend.

"You know why Hugo wears his hair so long, don't you, Pierrot?" asked Josette, turning to him. "It's because he has horns under there. If he got it cut, we'd all see them."

"Stop it," said Hugo, his tone not quite as fearless as before.

"I bet if you pulled his pants down, he'd have a tail, too."

"Stop it!" repeated Hugo, louder this time.

"Pierrot, you sleep in the same room as him. When he gets changed for bed, have you seen his tail?"

"It's really long and scaly," said Pierrot, feeling brave now that Josette was taking control of the conversation. "Like something a dragon would have."

"I don't think you should have to share with him at all," she said. "It's best not to mix with people like that. Everyone says so. There's a few of them in the orphanage. They should have their own room. Or be sent away."

"Shut *up!*" roared Hugo, advancing on her now, and she jumped back just as Pierrot stepped between them. The older boy's fists lashed out, catching Pierrot directly on the nose. There was a nasty crunching sound, and Pierrot fell to the ground, blood rushing down his upper lip. Josette screamed as Pierrot went *"Uuuurgh!"* and Hugo's mouth dropped open in surprise. A moment later he was gone, disappearing into the woods with Gérard and Marc running after him.

Pierrot could feel a strange sensation in his face. It wasn't entirely unpleasant; rather it was as if a really big sneeze was on its way. But a throbbing headache was forming behind his eyes, and his mouth felt very dry. He looked up at Josette, who had both hands pressed to her cheeks in shock.

"I'm fine," he said, standing up but feeling very weak in his legs as he did so. "It's just a scratch."

"It's not," said Josette. "We need to get you to the sisters right away."

"I'm fine," repeated Pierrot, putting a hand to his face to make sure everything was still where it was supposed to be. When he took it away again, however, his fingers were covered in blood, and he stared at them, his eyes opening wide. He remembered how Maman had taken the handkerchief away at her birthday dinner and it, too, had been spotted with blood. "That's not good," he said, before the whole forest started to spin, his legs grew weaker, and he fell to the ground, passing out cold.

When he woke, Pierrot was surprised to find himself lying on the sofa in the Durand sisters' office. Standing by the sink, Simone was holding a washcloth under running water before wringing it out. Stopping only to straighten a photograph on the wall, she came toward him and placed the cloth over the bridge of his nose.

"You're awake, then," she said.

"What happened?" asked Pierrot, propping himself up on his elbows. His head ached, his mouth felt dry, and there was an unpleasant burning sensation above his nose where Hugo had punched him.

"It's not broken," replied Simone, sitting down next to him. "I thought it was at first, but no. Although it will probably be quite sore for a few days, and you might have a black eye as the swelling goes down. If you're squeamish, you should probably avoid the mirror for a little while."

Pierrot swallowed and asked for a glass of water. In the months since he'd arrived at the orphanage, these were the most words Simone Durand had ever said to him. Usually, she barely spoke at all.

"I'll talk to Hugo," she said. "I'll tell him to apologize. And I'll make sure that nothing like this ever happens to you again."

"It wasn't Hugo," said Pierrot in an unconvincing tone, for despite the pain he was in, he still didn't like the idea of getting someone else in trouble.

"Yes, it was," replied Simone. "Josette told me, for one thing, although I would have guessed anyway."

"Why doesn't he like me?" he asked quietly, looking up at her.

"It's not your fault," she replied. "It's ours. Adèle's and mine. We've made mistakes with him. Many mistakes."

"But you take care of him," said Pierrot. "You look after all of us. And it's not as if any of us are your family. He should be grateful to you."

Simone tapped her fingers against the side of the chair as if she was weighing the importance of revealing a secret. "Actually, he *is* family," she said. "He's our nephew."

Pierrot opened his eyes wide in surprise. "Oh," he said. "I didn't know. I thought he was an orphan, just like the rest of us."

"His father died five years ago," she said. "And his mother . . ." She shook her head and wiped a tear from her eye. "Well, my parents treated her quite badly. They had some very silly, old-fashioned ideas about people. In the end, they drove her away. But Hugo's father was our brother, Jacques."

Pierrot glanced across at the picture of the two little girls standing hand in hand with the small boy, and the portrait of the man with the pencil mustache dressed in a French army uniform.

"What happened to him?" he asked.

"He died in jail. He'd been there since a few months before Hugo was born. He never even got to meet him."

Pierrot thought about this. He'd never known any-one who'd been to jail. He remembered reading about Philippe, the brother of King Louis XIII in *The Man in the Iron Mask*, who'd been falsely imprisoned in the Bastille; even the idea of such a fate had given him nightmares.

"Why was he in jail?" he asked.

"Our brother, like your father, fought in the Great War," Simone told him. "And while some men were able to return to their normal lives after the fighting ended, there were many—the vast majority, I believe—who were unable to cope with the memories of what they'd seen and what they'd done. Of course, there are doctors who have done everything they can to make the world understand the traumas of what took place twenty years ago. You only have to think of the work of Dr. Jules Persoinne here in France or Dr. Alfie Summerfield in England, who have made it their life's work to educate the public on how the previous generation suffered and how it is our responsibility to help them."

"My father was like that," said Pierrot. "Maman always said that although he didn't die in the Great War, it was the war that killed him."

"Yes," said Simone, nodding. "I understand what she meant. It was the same with Jacques. He was such a wonderful boy, so full of life and fun. The epitome of kindness. But afterward, when he came home . . . well, he was very different. And he did some terrible things. But he had served his country with honor." She stood up and walked across to the glass cabinet, opening the little latch at the front and removing the medal that Pierrot had stared at on the day he'd arrived. "Would you like to hold it?" she asked, holding it out.

The boy nodded and took it carefully in his hands, running his fingers across the figure that was molded onto the front.

"He was given that for bravery," she said, taking it back and replacing it in the cabinet. "That's all we have of him now. Over the decade that followed, he was in and out of jail on many occasions. Adèle and I visited often, but we hated it. To see him there in such horrible conditions, treated so badly by a country for which he had sacrificed his peace of mind. It was a tragedy—and not just for us but also for so many families. Yours included, Pierrot—am I right?"

He nodded but said nothing.

"Jacques died in prison and we've looked after Hugo ever since. A few years ago we talked to him about how our parents treated his mother and how our country treated his father. Perhaps he was too young and we should have waited until he was more mature. He has a great anger inside him now, and, unfortunately, that's something that manifests itself in his treatment of the other orphans. But you mustn't be too hard on him, Pierrot. Perhaps he picks on you the most because you are the one with whom he has the most in common."

Pierrot thought about this and tried to feel sympathy for Hugo, but it wasn't easy. After all, as Simone had pointed out, their fathers had gone through similar experiences, but *he* didn't go around making life miserable for everyone else.

"At least it came to an end," he said finally. "The war, I mean. There won't be another one, will there?"

"I hope not," replied Simone as the door to the office swung open and Adèle entered, brandishing a letter in her hand.

"There you are!" she said, looking from one to the other. "I've been looking for you both. What on earth happened to you?" she asked, leaning down and examining the bruises on Pierrot's face.

"I was in a fight," he said.

"Did you win?"

"No."

"Ah," she replied. "Hard luck. But I think this will cheer you up. You've had some good news. You're going to be leaving us soon."

Pierrot looked from one sister to the other in surprise. "A family wants me?" he asked.

"Not just *any* family," said Adèle, smiling. "*Your* family. Your *own* family, I mean."

"Adèle, will you please explain what's going on?" asked Simone, reaching to take the letter from her sister's hands and running her eyes across the envelope. "Austria?" she said in surprise, noticing the postmark.

"It's from your aunt Beatrix," said Adèle, looking at Pierrot.

"But I've never even met her!"

"Well, she knows all about you. You can read it. She's only recently found out about what happened to your mother. She wants you to go live with her."

Chapter

4

Three Train Journeys

Before waving him off at Orléans, Adèle handed Pierrot a pack of sandwiches and told him to eat them only when he was very hungry, as they had to last for the entire trip, which would take more than ten hours.

"Now, I've pinned the names of all three stops to your lapel," she added, fussing around him as she made sure that each scrap of paper was securely fastened to his coat. "And every time you arrive at a station whose name matches one of these, make sure you get off and change to the next train."

"Here," said Simone, reaching into her bag and passing a small gift across, neatly wrapped in brown paper. "We thought this might help to pass the time. It will remind you of the months you spent with us."

Pierrot kissed them both on the cheek, thanked them for all they had done for him, and boarded the train, choosing a train car where a woman and a young boy were already seated. The lady stared at him irritably as he sat down, as if she and the boy had hoped to have the train car entirely to themselves, but said nothing as she returned to her newspaper, while the boy picked up a packet of sweets from the seat next to him and put it in his pocket. Pierrot sat by the window as the train pulled out and waved at Simone and Adèle before looking down at the first note attached to his lapel. He read the word carefully to himself.

Mannheim.

He had said good-bye to his friends the previous night, and Josette had been the only one who seemed sorry to see him go.

"Are you sure you haven't found a family to adopt you?" she asked. "You're not just trying to make the rest of us feel better?"

"No," said Pierrot. "I can show you my aunt's letter if you like."

"So how did she track you down?"

"Anshel's mother was sorting through some of my mother's things, and she found the address. She wrote to tell Aunt Beatrix what had happened and gave her the details of the orphanage."

"And now she wants you to go live with her?"

"Yes," said Pierrot.

Josette shook her head. "Is she married?" she said.

"I don't think so."

"Then what does she do? How does she earn a living?"

"She's a housekeeper."

"A *housekeeper*?" asked Josette.

"Yes. What's wrong with that?"

"There's nothing *wrong* with it, Pierrot, *per se*," she replied, having read this phrase recently in a book and been determined ever since to find an opportunity to use it. "It's a little *bourgeois*, of course, but what can you do? And what about the family whose house she takes care of—what type of people are they?"

"It's not a family," said Pierrot. "It's just one man. And he said it was fine with him as long as I'm not noisy. He's not there very often, my aunt said."

"Well," said Josette, pretending to be indifferent but secretly wishing that she could go with him, "you can always come back, I suppose, if it doesn't work out."

Pierrot thought about this conversation now, as he watched the scenery fly past, and felt a little uncomfortable. It did seem strange that his aunt had never got in touch in all these years—after all, she had missed seven birthdays and Christmases during that time—but of course it was possible that she didn't get along with Maman, particularly after everything that had happened between Beatrix and Pierrot's father. He tried to put his concerns out of his mind for now, however, and closed his eyes for a little snooze, only opening them again when an elderly man entered the train car to take the fourth and final seat. Pierrot sat up straight, stretched his arms, and yawned as he glanced across at him. The man was wearing a long black coat, black trousers, and a white shirt, and he had long dark curls on either side of his head. He obviously had some difficulty walking, too, because he used a cane.

"Oh, now this is too much," said the lady opposite, closing her newspaper and shaking her head. She was speaking German, and something in Pierrot's head realigned itself to recall the language that he had always spoken with his father. "Really, can't you find anywhere else to sit?"

The man shook his head. "Madam, the train is full," he said politely. "And here is an empty seat."

"No, I'm sorry," she snapped, "but this just won't do."

And with that, she stood up and left the train car, marching down the corridor while Pierrot looked around in surprise, wondering how she could possibly object to someone sitting with them when there was a place available. The man looked out the window for a moment and sighed deeply, but he didn't put his case on the rack above, even though it was taking up a lot of space between them.

"Would you like some help with that?" asked Pierrot. "I can put it up there if you like."

The man smiled and shook his head. "I think you would be wasting your time," he said. "But you're very kind to offer."

The woman now returned with the conductor, who looked around the train car and pointed toward the old man. "Come on, you," he said. "Out. You can stand in the corridor."

"But the seat is empty," said Pierrot, who assumed the conductor thought that his mother or father was traveling with him and that the old man had taken their seat. "I'm alone."

"Out. Now," insisted the conductor, ignoring Pierrot. "On your feet, old man, or there'll be trouble."

The man said nothing and stood up, planting his cane carefully on the ground as he picked up his suitcase and, with great dignity, navigated his way slowly through the door.

"I'm sorry about that, madam," said the conductor, turning to the lady when the man was gone.

"You should be watching out for them," she snapped. "I have my son with me. He shouldn't be exposed to people like that."

"I'm sorry," he repeated, and the woman snorted in disgust, as if the entire world were conspiring to frustrate her.

Pierrot wanted to ask her why she had made the man

leave, but he found her a frightening presence and thought that if he said anything, he might have to go, too. So, instead, he turned away and looked out the window, closing his eyes once again, and started to doze.

When he awoke, the compartment door was being opened and the woman and the boy were taking down their bags.

"Where are we?" he asked.

"Germany," she said, smiling for the first time. "Finally away from all those awful French people!" She pointed toward a sign that, like Pierrot's lapel, said *Mannheim*. "This is where you get off, I think," she added, nodding toward his jacket, and he jumped up, gathered his belongings, and made his way out to the platform.

Standing in the center of the station concourse, Pierrot felt anxious and alone. Everywhere he looked, men and women were hurrying along, brushing past him, desperate to get to wherever they were going. And soldiers, too. Lots and lots of soldiers.

The first thing he noticed, however, was how the language had changed. They had crossed the border, and everyone was now talking in German instead of French, and as he listened carefully, trying to understand what people were saying, he was glad that Papa had insisted on his learning the language as a child. He tore the

Mannheim sticker off his jacket, threw it in the nearest wastebasket, and looked down to read what the next one said:

Munich.

An enormous clock hung over the arrivals and departures board. He ran toward it, crashing into a man walking toward him, and fell backward onto the ground. Looking up, his eyes took in the man's earth-gray uniform and the heavy black belt he wore across his waist, the calf-high black jackboots and the patch on his left sleeve that showed an eagle with its wings outstretched over a hooked cross.

"I'm sorry," he said breathlessly, looking up with a mixture of fear and awe.

The man looked down, and rather than helping him up, curled his lip in contempt as he raised the tip of one boot slightly, pressing it down on top of Pierrot's fingers.

"You're hurting me," he cried as the man pushed down harder, and now he could feel his fingers begin to throb beneath the pressure. He had never seen someone take so much pleasure from inflicting pain before. Even though the passing commuters could see what was happening, no one stepped in to help.

"There you are, Ralf," said a woman, approaching him now, carrying a little boy in her arms as a girl about five years old followed behind. "I'm so sorry, but Bruno wanted to see the steam trains and we almost lost you. Oh, what's happened here?" she asked as the man smiled, lifted his boot, and reached down to help Pierrot up.

"A child running along and not watching where he was going," he said with a shrug. "He almost knocked me over."

"His clothes are so old," said the girl, looking Pierrot up and down distastefully.

"Gretel, I've told you before about making such remarks," said the girl's mother, frowning.

"They smell, too."

"Gretel!"

"Shall we go?" asked the man, glancing at his watch, and his wife nodded.

They marched away, and Pierrot watched their retreating backs, massaging the fingers of one hand with the fingers of the other. As he did so, the little boy turned around in his mother's arms and raised a hand to wave good-bye, and their eyes met. Despite the pain in his knuckles, Pierrot couldn't help but smile, and he waved back. As they disappeared into the crowd, the whistles blew all around the station, and Pierrot realized that he needed to find the right train quickly or he might end up stuck in Mannheim.

The board showed that his train was shortly to depart from Platform Three, and he ran toward it, jumping aboard just as the conductor started to slam the doors. The next journey, he knew, would take three hours, and by now the excitement of being on a train had well and truly worn off.

The train shuddered as it left the station in a cloud of steam and noise, and he watched from the open window as a woman wearing a head scarf and dragging a suitcase behind her ran toward it, calling to the driver to wait. Three soldiers huddled together on the platform started laughing at her; Pierrot watched as she put her bag down and began to argue with them, but he was shocked when one reached out, grabbed her arm, and twisted it behind her back. He only had time to watch the expression on the woman's face change from fury to agony before a hand tapped him on the shoulder and he spun around.

"What are you doing out here?" said the conductor. "Do you have a ticket?"

Pierrot reached into his pocket and took out all the documents that the Durand sisters had given him before leaving the orphanage. The man flicked through them roughly, and Pierrot watched as his ink-stained fingers ran across the lines, his lips mouthing each word to himself under his breath. He stank of cigar smoke, and Pierrot felt his stomach lunge a little with the combination of the bad smell and the movement of the train.

"All right, then," the conductor said, thrusting the tickets back into Pierrot's jacket pocket and peering at the place names on his lapel. "You're traveling alone, are you?"

"Yes, sir."

"No parents?"

"No, sir."

"Well, you can't stand out here while the train is in motion. It's dangerous. You could fall out and be turned into mincemeat under the wheels. Don't think it hasn't happened before. A boy your size wouldn't stand a chance."

Pierrot felt these words like a knife going through his heart—for this, after all, was how Papa had died.

"Come along, then," said the man, grabbing him roughly by the shoulders and dragging him past a row of compartments as Pierrot carried his suitcase and sandwiches with him. "Full," muttered the conductor, looking into one before moving on quickly. "Full," he said again when he saw the next one. "Full. Full. Full." He glanced down at Pierrot. "There might not be a seat," he said. "The train is packed today, so you might not be able to sit. But you can't stand all the way to Munich, either. It's a safety concern."

Pierrot said nothing. He didn't know what this

meant. If he couldn't sit and he couldn't stand, then that didn't leave him a lot of alternatives. It wasn't as if he could float.

"Ah," said the man finally, opening a door and looking inside. A buzz of laughter and conversation spilled out into the corridor. "There's room for a small one in here. You don't mind, boys, do you? We have a child traveling on his own to Munich. I'll leave him in here for you to look after."

The conductor stepped out of the way, and Pierrot felt his anxiety grow even more. Five boys, all aged around fourteen or fifteen, well-built, blond, and clear-skinned, turned to look at him silently, as if they were a pack of hungry wolves unexpectedly alerted to fresh prey.

"Come in, little man," said one, the tallest of the group, indicating the empty seat between the two boys opposite him. "We won't bite." He held his hand out and beckoned him forward slowly. There was something about the movement that made Pierrot feel very uncomfortable. But having no choice, he sat down, and within a few minutes the boys had started talking to one another again and ignoring him. Pierrot felt very small seated among them.

For a long time he stared at his shoes, but after a while, when his confidence grew, he raised his eyes from the floor and pretended to look out the window. In reality he was staring at just one boy, who was snoozing with his head pressed against the glass. All the boys were dressed alike in uniforms of brown shirts, black shorts, black ties, white kneesocks, and diamond-shaped armbands, colored red at the upper and lower sections and white at the left and right. In the center was the same hooked cross as the one on the sleeve of the man who had stood on his fingers at the Mannheim station. Pierrot couldn't help but be impressed, and he wished he had a uniform like theirs instead of the secondhand clothes the Durand sisters had given him back at the orphanage. If he were dressed like these boys, then strange girls in train stations wouldn't be able to make remarks about how old his clothes were.

"My father was a soldier," he said suddenly, surprising himself with how loudly the words emerged from his mouth. The boys stopped talking to one another and stared at him, while the boy by the window woke up and blinked a few times, looking around and asking whether they'd arrived at Munich yet.

"What was that you said, little man?" asked the first boy, the obvious leader of their group.

"I said that my father was a soldier," repeated Pierrot, already regretting having said anything at all.

"And when was this?"

"During the war."

"Your accent," said the boy, leaning forward. "Your

language skills are good, but you're not a native German, are you?"

Pierrot shook his head.

"Let me guess." A smile crossed his face as he pointed a finger at Pierrot's heart. "Swiss. No, French! I'm right, amn't I?"

Pierrot nodded.

The boy raised an eyebrow and then sniffed the air a few times as if he were trying to identify an unpleasant smell. "And how old are you. Six?"

"I'm seven," said Pierrot, sitting up straight, mortally offended.

"You're too small to be seven."

"I know," said Pierrot. "But someday I'll be bigger."

"Perhaps, if you live that long. And where are you going?"

"To meet my aunt," said Pierrot.

"And is she French, too?"

"No, she's German."

The boy considered this and offered him an unsettling smile. "Do you know how I feel right now, little man?" he asked.

"No," said Pierrot.

"Hungry."

"Didn't you have any breakfast today?" he asked, which led to uproarious laughter from two of the other

66

boys, who stopped laughing almost immediately when their leader glared at them.

"Yes, I had breakfast," he replied calmly. "I had a delicious breakfast, actually. And I had lunch. I even had a little snack at the Mannheim station. But I'm still hungry."

Pierrot glanced down at the pack of sandwiches sitting on the seat next to him, and he regretted not having put them in his suitcase with the gift that Simone had given him. He'd been planning on eating two here and saving the last one for the final train.

"Maybe there's a shop on board," he said.

"But I have no money," said the boy, smiling and extending his arms. "I'm just a young man in the service of the Fatherland. A mere Rottenführer, the son of a literature professor—although, yes, I am superior to these lowly and wretched members of the Hitlerjugend you see beside me. Is your father wealthy?"

"My father is dead."

"Did he die during the war?"

"No. Afterward."

The boy considered this. "I bet your mother is very pretty," he said, reaching out for a moment and touching Pierrot's face.

"My mother is dead, too," Pierrot replied, pulling away.

"What a pity. I assume she was also French?"

"Yes."

"Then it doesn't matter so much."

"Come on, Kurt," said the boy by the window. "Leave him alone. He's just a kid."

"Do you have something to say, Schlenheim?" he snapped, turning his head in one quick movement and staring at his friend. "And did you forget your etiquette while you were snoring like a pig over there?"

Schlenheim swallowed nervously and shook his head. "I apologize, Rottenführer Kotler," he said quietly, his face turning red. "I spoke out of turn."

"Then I repeat," said Kotler, looking back at Pierrot, "I'm hungry. If only there was something to eat. But wait! What's this?" He smiled, showing an even set of sparkling white teeth. "Are those sandwiches?" He reached across and picked up Pierrot's pack and sniffed it. "I believe they are. Someone must have left them behind."

"They're mine," said Pierrot.

"Is your name written on them?"

"You can't write your name on bread," said Pierrot.

"In that case, we can't be sure that they are yours. And having found them, I claim them as my prize." And with that, Kotler opened the packet, took out the first sandwich, and devoured it in three quick bites before starting on the second. "Delicious," he said, offering the last one to Schlenheim, who shook his head. "Aren't you hungry?" he asked.

"No, Rottenführer Kotler."

"I'm sure I can hear your stomach grumbling. Eat one."

Schlenheim reached out to take the sandwich, his hands trembling a little as he did so.

"Very good," said Kotler, smiling. "I'm sorry there wasn't another," he said, shrugging his shoulders at Pierrot. "If there had been, I could have given one to you. You look as if you're starving!"

Pierrot stared at him and wanted to tell him exactly what he thought of thieves older than he was stealing his food, but there was something about this boy that made him understand that he would come off worse in any exchange they might have, and it wasn't just because Kotler was bigger. Pierrot could feel tears forming behind his eyes but promised himself that he wouldn't cry, blinking instead to force them to retreat as he looked down at the floor. Kotler inched his boot forward slowly, and when Pierrot looked up, he tossed the crumpled, empty bag at him, hitting him in the face, before returning to his conversation with the boys around him.

And from there to Munich, Pierrot never opened his mouth again.

When the train pulled into the station a couple of hours later, the members of the Hitlerjugend collected their belongings, but Pierrot held back, waiting for them to leave first. They walked out one by one until only Pierrot and Rottenführer Kotler remained. The older boy glanced down at him and bent over, examining the place name on his lapel. "You must get off here," he said. "This is your stop." He spoke as if he hadn't bullied him at all but was merely being helpful as he ripped the piece of paper from Pierrot's coat before leaning over to read the final note:

Salzburg.

"Ah," he said. "You are not staying in Germany, I see. You're traveling on to Austria."

A sudden panic entered Pierrot's mind when he thought about his final destination, and although he really didn't want to converse with this boy anymore, he knew that he had to ask. "You're not going there, too, are you?" he asked, dreading the idea that they might end up on the same train again.

"What, to Austria?" asked Kotler, taking his knapsack from above the seat and making his way through the door. He smiled and shook his head. "No," he said. He started to move on, thought better of it, and looked back. "At least, not yet," he added with a wink. "But soon. Very soon, I think. Today the Austrian people have a place they call home. But one day . . . *poof!*" He pressed the tips of his fingers together and pulled them apart, making the sound of an explosion, before bursting into laughter as he disappeared out of the compartment and onto the platform beyond.

The final journey to Salzburg took less than two hours. By now Pierrot was tired and very hungry, but as exhausted as he felt, he was afraid of falling asleep in case he missed his stop. He thought of the map of Europe that hung on the wall of his classroom in Paris and tried to imagine where he might end up if that happened. Russia, perhaps. Or farther away still.

He was alone in the train car now and, remembering the present that Simone had handed him on the platform at Orléans, he reached into his suitcase and took it out, unwrapping the brown paper and running his finger beneath the words on the cover of the book.

Emil and the Detectives, it said. *By Erich Kästner.*

The illustration on the front showed a man walking down a yellow street while two boys peered out at him from behind a pillar. In the lower right-hand corner was the word *Trier*. He read the opening lines:

"Now then, Emil," Mrs. Tischbein said, "just carry in that jug of hot water for me, will you?" She picked up one jug and a little blue bowl of liquid chamomile shampoo, and hurried out of the kitchen into the front room. Emil took his jug and followed her.

Before long, he was surprised to discover that the boy in the book, Emil, had a few things in common with him—or at least with the person he used to be. Emil lives alone with his mother—although in Berlin, not Paris—and his father is dead. And early in the novel, Emil, like Pierrot, goes on a train journey, and a man seated in his train car steals his money, just as Rottenführer Kotler had stolen his sandwiches. Pierrot was glad that he didn't have any money, but he had a suitcase filled with clothes, his toothbrush, a photograph of his parents, and a new story that Anshel had sent him just before he left the orphanage, which he had already read twice. It was about a boy who was the subject of name-calling from people he used to think of as his friends, and Pierrot found the whole thing a little disturbing. He preferred the stories Anshel had written before, about magicians and talking animals. He moved his suitcase closer to him now in case anyone came in and did to him what Max Grundeis had done to Emil. Finally the motion of the train became so soothing that he could no longer keep his eyes open, the book slipped from his hands, and he dozed off.

In what felt like only a few moments, he jumped as a loud rapping on the window woke him up. He looked around in surprise, wondering for a moment where he was, and then panicking that he had arrived in Russia after all. The train had come to a stop and there was an eerie silence.

The knocking came again, sharper this time, but there was so much condensation on the glass that he couldn't see out to the platform. Sweeping his hand across it in a perfect arc, he cleared a section that allowed him to see an enormous sign—which, to his relief, read *Salzburg*. A rather beautiful woman with long red hair was standing outside looking in at him. She was saying something, but he couldn't make out the words. She said it again—still nothing. He reached up, opened the small window at the top, and now her words carried through to him at last.

"Pierrot," she cried. "It's me! I'm your aunt Beatrix!"

Chapter

5

The House at the Top
of the Mountain

Pierrot woke the next morning to find himself in an
unfamiliar room. The ceiling was made up of a series of
long wooden beams crisscrossed by darker columns,
and inhabiting the corner of the plank above his head
was a large spiderweb whose architect hung menacingly
by a rotating silken thread.

He lay still for a few minutes, trying to recall more
about the journey that had brought him there. The last
thing he remembered was getting off the train and walking along the platform with a woman who said she was
his aunt, before climbing into the back of a car driven by
a man wearing a dark gray uniform and a chauffeur's
cap. After that, everything went dark. He had a vague
idea that he had mentioned how one of the boys from
the Hitlerjugend had bullied him out of his sandwiches.
The chauffeur had said something about the way those

boys behaved, but Aunt Beatrix had silenced him quickly, and soon he must have fallen asleep—to dream that he was soaring into the clouds, higher and higher, growing colder by the minute. And then a pair of strong arms had lifted him from the car and carried him through to a bedroom, where a woman tucked him in and kissed him on the forehead before turning out the lights.

He sat up now and looked around. The room was quite small—smaller even than the one he had slept in at home in Paris—and contained nothing more than the bed he was lying in, a chest of drawers with a bowl and jug on top, and a wardrobe in the corner. He lifted the sheets, looked down, and was surprised to see that he was wearing a long nightshirt with nothing underneath it. Someone must have undressed him, and the idea of this made his face grow red because whoever it was would have seen *everything*.

Pierrot climbed out of bed and walked over to the wardrobe, his bare feet cold against the wooden floor below, but his clothes were not inside. He opened the drawers of the chest, but they were empty, too. The jug was full of water, however, so he drank a little and swirled it around in his mouth, and then poured a little into the bowl so he could wash his face. Walking over to the single window, he pulled the curtain back to look outside, but the glass was frosted over and he could only make out an indistinct blend of green and white beyond, which suggested a field working hard to break through the snow. He felt a twist of anxiety build in his stomach.

Where am I? he wondered.

Turning around, he noticed a portrait on the wall of an extremely serious man with a small mustache staring into the distance; he was wearing a yellow jacket and an iron cross on his breast pocket, one hand resting on the top of a chair, the other pressed against his hip. Behind him hung a painting of trees and a sky that was darkening with gray clouds, as if a terrible storm was brewing.

Pierrot found himself staring at the painting for a long time—there was something hypnotic about the man's expression—and he only snapped out of it when he heard footsteps making their way along the corridor outside. Quickly, he jumped back into bed and pulled the sheets up to his chin. When the door handle turned, a rather portly girl of about eighteen years of age, with red hair and an even redder face, looked inside.

"You're awake, then," she said in an accusatory tone.

Pierrot said nothing, simply nodded.

"You're to come with me," she said.

"Where to?"

"Where I take you, that's where. Come on. Hurry up. I'm busy enough as it is without having to answer a lot of silly questions."

Pierrot climbed out of bed and walked toward her, looking down at his feet instead of directly at her. "Where are my clothes?" he asked.

"Gone into the incinerator," she said. "They'll be ashes by now."

Pierrot gasped in dismay. The clothes he had worn for the journey were clothes that Maman had bought for him on his seventh birthday; it was the last occasion they had gone shopping together.

"And my suitcase?" he asked.

She shrugged but didn't look the least bit remorseful. "Everything's gone," she said. "We didn't want those nasty, smelly things in the house."

"But they—" began Pierrot.

"You can stop that nonsense right now," said the girl, turning around and wagging a finger in his face. "They were filthy and most likely crawling with undesirables. They're better off in the fire. And you're lucky to be here in the Berghof—"

"The what?" asked Pierrot.

"The Berghof," she repeated. "That's what this house is called. And we don't allow tantrums here. Now, follow me. I don't want to hear another word out of you."

He walked along the corridor, looking left and right, trying to take everything in. The house was made almost entirely of wood, and although it felt pretty and cozy, the photographs on the walls showing groups of officers in uniforms standing at attention—some looking directly down the camera lens as if they were hoping to intimidate it into cracking—seemed a little out of place. He stood in front of one of them, mesmerized by what he saw. The men looked fierce, frightening, handsome, and electrifying all at once. Pierrot wondered whether he might look as frightening as they did when he was grown up; then no one would dare to knock him over in train stations or steal his sandwiches on the train.

"She takes those photos," said the girl, stopping when she saw what Pierrot was looking at.

"Who?" he asked.

"The mistress. Now, stop dawdling—the water's getting cold."

Pierrot didn't know what she meant by this but followed her as she made her way down the staircase and turned left.

"What's your name again?" she asked, looking back at him. "I can't get it straight in my head."

"Pierrot," said Pierrot.

"What sort of name is that?"

"I don't know," he said, shrugging his shoulders. "It's just my name."

"Don't shrug," she said. "The mistress can't abide people who shrug. She says it's common."

"Do you mean my aunt?" asked Pierrot.

The girl stopped and stared at him for a moment

before throwing her head back and laughing. "Beatrix isn't the mistress," she said. "She's just the housekeeper. The mistress is . . . Well, she's the mistress, isn't she? She's in charge. Your aunt takes her orders from her. We all do."

"What's your name?" asked Pierrot.

"Herta Theissen," said the girl. "I'm the second-most senior of the maids here."

"How many are there?"

"Two," she replied. "But the mistress says we'll need more soon, and when the others come, I'll still be second and they'll answer to me."

"And do you live here, too?" he asked.

"Of course I do. Do you think I just popped in for the good of my health? There's the master and mistress when they're here, although we haven't seen them in a few weeks now. Sometimes they come for a weekend and sometimes for longer, and then sometimes we might not see them for a whole month. Then there's Emma—she's the cook, and you don't want to get on the wrong side of her. And Ute, the senior maid. Ernst, the chauffeur, of course. You met him last night, I expect. Oh, he's wonderful! So handsome and funny and thoughtful." She stopped talking for a few moments and sighed happily. "And there's your aunt, of course. The housekeeper. There's usually a couple of soldiers at the door, but they change too often for us to bother getting to know them."

"Where is my aunt?" asked Pierrot, already deciding that he didn't like Herta very much.

"She's gone down the mountain with Ernst to pick up a few necessities. She'll be back soon, I expect. Although you never know with that pair. Your aunt has a terrible habit of wasting his time. I'd say something to her about it, only she has seniority over me and would probably report me to the mistress."

Herta opened another door, and Pierrot followed her in. A tin bathtub stood in the center of the room, half filled with water, steam rising from the surface.

"Is it wash day?" he asked.

"It is for you," said Herta, rolling up her sleeves. "Come on, get that nightshirt off and climb in so I can scrub you clean. God only knows what kind of dirt you've brought with you. I never met a Frenchman who wasn't filthy."

"Oh no," said Pierrot, shaking his head and backing away, holding both palms out in the air to stop her from getting anywhere near him. There was no way he was going to take his clothes off in front of a complete stranger—and especially not in front of a girl. He hadn't even liked doing that in the orphanage, and there were only boys in the dormitory there. "No, no, no. Absolutely not. I'm not taking anything off. Sorry, but no."

"Do you think you have a choice in this?" asked Herta, putting her hands on her hips and staring at him as if he were a member of an alien species. "Orders are orders, Pierre—"

"Pierrot."

"You'll learn that soon enough. Orders are given and we obey them. Every time and without question."

"I won't do it," said Pierrot, growing red with embarrassment. "Even my mother stopped bathing me when I was five."

"Well, your mother's dead—that's what I heard. And your father jumped under a train."

Pierrot stared at her, unable to say anything for a moment. He couldn't quite believe that anyone would say something so cruel.

"I'll wash myself," he said finally, his voice cracking a little. "I know how to do it, and I'll do it right. I promise."

Herta threw her hands in the air in defeat. "Fine," she said, picking up a square of soap and slamming it sharply into the palm of his hand. "But I'll be back in fifteen minutes, and I want all that soap to be used up by then, do you understand me? Otherwise, I'll take the scrubbing brush to you myself, and there's nothing you can say that will stop me."

Pierrot nodded and breathed a sigh of relief, waiting until she had left the bathroom before taking off the nightshirt and climbing carefully into the bath. Once he was in, he lay back and closed his eyes, enjoying the unexpected luxury. It had been a long time since he'd taken a warm bath. In the orphanage, they were always cold, as there were so many children who needed to use the same water. He softened the soap, and when it produced a good lather, he began to wash himself.

The bathwater quickly turned murky from all the dirt that had collected on his body, and he buried his head under the surface, enjoying the way the sounds of the outside world disappeared, before massaging his scalp with the soap to wash his hair. When he'd rinsed out all the lather, he sat up and scrubbed his feet and his fingernails. To his relief, the soap got smaller and smaller, but he kept washing until it disappeared entirely, relieved that when Herta returned she would have no cause to go through with her appalling threat.

When she came back in—without even knocking!— she was carrying a large towel, and held it out before him. "Come on, then," she said. "Out you get."

"Turn around," said Pierrot.

"Oh, for pity's sake," said Herta with a sigh, turning her head away and closing her eyes. Pierrot climbed out of the bath and allowed himself to be enveloped in the fabric, which was softer and more sumptuous than any he had ever known. It felt so comfortable wrapped tightly around his small body that he would have been happy to stay in it forever.

"Right," said Herta. "I've left fresh clothes on your

bed. They're too big for you, but they'll have to do for now. Beatrix is going to take you down the mountain to get you new clothes, or so I'm told."

The mountain again.

"Why am I on a mountain?" asked Pierrot. "What sort of place is this?"

"No more questions," said Herta, turning away. "I have things to do even if you don't. Get dressed, and when you come downstairs, you can find something to eat if you're hungry."

Pierrot ran back upstairs to his room still wrapped in the towel, his feet leaving small outlines on the wooden floor, and sure enough, a set of clothes had been laid out neatly on his bed. He put them on, rolling up the sleeves of the shirt, turning up the cuffs on the trousers and fastening the suspenders as tightly as he could. There was a heavy sweater, too, but it was so oversized that when he put it on, it hung down below his knees. He took it off again and decided to brave the weather.

Walking back downstairs, he looked around, uncertain where he was supposed to go now, but there was no one around to help him.

"Hello?" he said quietly, nervous about drawing too much attention to himself but hoping that someone would hear. "Hello?" he repeated, walking toward the front door. He could hear voices out there—two men laughing—and turned the handle, opening it to reveal a burst of sunlight despite the cold. As he stepped outside, the men threw their half-smoked cigarettes on the ground, crushing them underfoot, standing tall and staring directly ahead. A pair of living statues wearing gray uniforms, gray peaked caps, heavy black belts around their waists, and dark black boots that reached almost to their knees.

They both carried rifles slung over their shoulders.

"Good morning," said Pierrot cautiously.

Neither soldier spoke, so he walked out a little farther before turning around and looking from one to the other; but still neither of them said a word. A sense of their ridiculousness overtook him and he put two fingers to the corners of his mouth, stretched his lips as wide as he could and rolled his eyes, trying not to giggle too much. They didn't react. He hopped up and down on one foot while slapping a hand back and forth against his mouth, letting out a war cry. Still nothing.

"I am Pierrot!" he declared. "King of the mountain!"

Now the head of one of the soldiers turned a little, and the expression on his face, the manner in which his lip curled and his shoulder lifted slightly, causing his rifle to rise, too, made Pierrot think that maybe he shouldn't talk to them anymore.

A part of him wanted to go back inside and find something to eat, as Herta had suggested. He hadn't eaten anything in the twenty-four hours since leaving

Orléans. But for now he was too intent on looking around, trying to discover exactly where he was. He walked across the grass, which had a white frosting that crackled in a pleasing manner beneath his boots, and looked out at the view. The sight that he beheld was astonishing. He wasn't just at the top of a mountain; he was on a mountain within a collection of other mountains, each one with huge peaks that rose into the clouds. Their snowy summits mingled with the white of the sky, and the clouds gathered between them, disguising where one ended and the next began. Pierrot had never seen anything quite like this in his life. He made his way around to the other side of the house and looked at the landscape from there.

It was beautiful. An enormous, silent world captured in tranquillity.

He heard a sound in the distance and wandered around the perimeter, staring down at the winding road that led from the front of the house through the heart of the mountains, twisting left and right in unpredictable ways before blurring into the invisible area below. How far up was he? he wondered. He breathed in, and the air felt so fresh and light, filling his lungs and his spirit with an enormous sense of well-being. Looking back down at the road, he watched as a car worked its way toward him and wondered whether he ought to go back inside before whoever was in it arrived. He wished Anshel were here; he would know what to do. They had written regularly to each other when Pierrot was in the orphanage, but the move had happened so quickly that he didn't even have time to let his friend know. He would have to write soon, but what address would he offer?

Pierrot Fischer
The Top of the Mountain
Somewhere near Salzburg

That would hardly do.

The car drew closer and stopped at a checkpoint about twenty feet below. Pierrot watched as a soldier emerged from a little wooden hut before lifting the barrier and waving it forward. It was the same car that had collected him from the train station the night before, the black Volkswagen with the retractable roof, a pair of black, white, and red flags blowing in the breeze at the front. When it pulled up, Ernst got out and walked around to open the back door, and Pierrot's aunt stepped out, the two of them chatting for a moment before she glanced in the direction of the soldiers at the door, then seemed to rearrange her face into a stern expression. Ernst went back and climbed into the driver's seat, then drove forward to park a little distance away.

Beatrix asked something of one of the soldiers, who pointed in Pierrot's direction, and she turned and caught his eye. As her face relaxed into a smile, he thought how much like his father she was. Her expression reminded him deeply of Wilhelm, and he wished that he were back in Paris, in the good old days when his parents were both alive and had cared for him and loved him and kept him safe while D'Artagnan scratched at the door longing for a walk and Anshel was downstairs ready to teach Pierrot silent words through fingers and thumbs.

Beatrix raised a hand in the air, and he waited for a moment before raising his own in reply and walking over, growing curious now as to what his new life would entail.

Chapter

6

A Little Less French, a Little More German

The following morning, Beatrix came into Pierrot's bedroom to tell him that they were going to take a trip down the mountain to buy him some new clothes.

"The things you brought with you from Paris were not suitable for here," she said, glancing around and walking over to close the door. "The master has very strict ideas about such things. And it will be safer for you to wear traditional German clothing anyway. Your own clothes were a little too bohemian for his tastes."

"Safer?" asked Pierrot, surprised by her choice of words.

"It wasn't easy to persuade him to let you come here," she explained. "He's not accustomed to children. I had to promise that you would be no trouble."

"Doesn't he have any of his own?" Pierrot had hoped

that there might be another child his own age who would come when the master did.

"No. And it would be best if you didn't do anything to upset him, in case he decides to send you back to Orléans."

"The orphanage wasn't as bad as I thought it would be," said Pierrot. "Simone and Adèle were very kind to me."

"I'm sure they were. But it's family that matters. And you and I are family. The only family that either one of us has left. We must never let each other down."

Pierrot nodded, but there was one thing that he had been thinking about ever since his aunt's letter arrived. "Why did we never meet until now?" he asked. "How come you never visited Papa, Maman, and me in Paris?"

Beatrix shook her head and stood up. "That's not a story for today," she said. "But we'll talk about it another time if you like. Now, come along, you must be hungry."

After breakfast, they made their way outside to where Ernst was leaning casually against the car, reading a newspaper. When he looked up and saw them, he smiled and folded it in half, placing it under his arm and opening the back door. Pierrot glanced at his uniform—how smart it looked!—and wondered whether his aunt might be persuaded to buy him something like that. He'd always liked uniforms. His father had kept one in a wardrobe in their Paris apartment—an apple-green cloth tunic with a rounded collar, six buttons running down the center, and trousers to match—but never wore it. Once, when Papa caught Pierrot trying on the jacket, he had frozen in the doorway, unable to move, and Maman had scolded her son for rooting around in things that were not his.

"Good morning, Pierrot!" said the chauffeur cheerfully, tousling the boy's hair. "Did you sleep well?"

"Very well, thank you."

"I had a dream last night that I was playing football for Germany," said Ernst. "I scored the winning goal against the English, and everyone cheered as I was carried off the field on the shoulders of the other players."

Pierrot nodded. He didn't like it when people recounted their dreams. Like some of Anshel's more complicated stories, they never really made any sense.

"Where to, Fräulein Fischer?" Ernst asked, bowing low before Beatrix and tipping his cap dramatically.

She laughed as she climbed into the backseat. "I must have received a promotion, Pierrot," she said. "Ernst never refers to me in such respectful terms. Into town, please. Pierrot needs new clothes."

"Don't listen to her," said Ernst, taking his place in the driver's seat and turning the ignition on. "Your aunt knows how highly I think of her."

Pierrot turned to look at Beatrix, whose eyes were meeting the chauffeur's in the rearview mirror, and noticed the half smile that lit up her face and the slight flush of red that appeared on her cheeks. As they drove off, he glanced around through the back window and got a view of the house as it disappeared from sight. It was very beautiful, its blond wooden frame standing out amid the rugged, snowy landscape like an unexpected charm.

"I remember the first time I saw it," Beatrix said, following the direction of his eyes. "I couldn't believe how tranquil it was. I felt certain that this would be a place of great serenity."

"It is," muttered Ernst under his breath, but loud enough for Pierrot to hear. "When *he's* not around."

"How long have you lived here?" asked Pierrot, turning back to his aunt.

"Well, I was thirty-four when I first arrived, so it must be . . . oh, a little over two years now."

Pierrot examined her carefully. She was very beautiful, that much was obvious, with long red hair that curled up a little around her shoulders and pale, unblemished skin. "So you're thirty-six?" he asked after a moment. "That's so old!"

"Ha!" cried Beatrix, bursting out laughing.

"Pierrot, you and I need to have a little talk," said Ernst. "If you're ever going to find a girlfriend, you need to know how to speak to one. You must never tell a woman that she looks old. Always guess five years younger than you really think."

"I don't want a girlfriend," said Pierrot quickly, appalled by the idea.

"You say that now. Let's see how you feel in a few years' time."

Pierrot shook his head. He remembered his friend Anshel going all silly over a new girl in their class, writing stories for her and leaving flowers on her desk. He'd had to have a serious talk with his friend about it, but there was nothing he could do to change his mind; Anshel was smitten. The whole thing had seemed utterly ridiculous to Pierrot.

"How old are you, Ernst?" asked Pierrot, leaning forward and moving his body into the gap between the two front seats to get a better look at the chauffeur.

"I'm twenty-seven," said Ernst, glancing back at him. "I know, it's impossible to believe. I look like a boy in the first flush of youth."

"Eyes on the road, Ernst," said Aunt Beatrix quietly, but her tone betrayed her amusement. "And sit back, Pierrot. It's dangerous to sit like that. If we hit a bump—"

"Are you going to marry Herta?" asked Pierrot, interrupting her.

"Herta? Which Herta?"

"The maid at the house."

"Herta Theissen?" asked Ernst, raising his voice in horror. "Good God, no. Why on earth would you think that?"

"She said you were handsome and funny and thoughtful."

Beatrix burst out laughing and covered her mouth with her hands. "Can it be true, Ernst?" she asked, teasing him. "Is the mild-mannered Herta in love with you?"

"Women are always falling in love with me," said Ernst with a shrug. "It's a cross I have to bear. They take one look at me and that's it. They're lost forever." He clicked his fingers. "It's not easy being this handsome, you know."

"Or that humble," added Beatrix.

"Perhaps she likes your uniform," suggested Pierrot.

"Every girl likes a man in uniform," said Ernst.

"Every girl, perhaps," remarked Beatrix. "But not every uniform."

"You know why people wear uniforms, don't you, Pierrot?" continued the chauffeur.

The boy shook his head.

"Because a person who wears one believes he can do anything he likes."

"Ernst," said Beatrix quietly.

"He can treat others in a way he never would while wearing normal clothes. Collars, trench coats, or jackboots, uniforms allow us to exercise our cruelty without ever feeling guilt."

"Ernst, that's enough," insisted Beatrix.

"You don't think I'm right?"

"You know I do," said Beatrix. "But this isn't the time for such a conversation."

Ernst said nothing and drove on silently while Pierrot considered what he had said and tried to make sense of it. He didn't really agree with him. He loved uniforms and wished he had one of his own. "Are there any children to play with here?" he asked after a moment.

"I'm afraid not," said Beatrix. "In the town, yes, there are many. And, of course, you'll start school soon, so I daresay you'll make some friends there."

"Will they be able to come to the mountaintop to play?"

"No, the master wouldn't like that."

"We'll have to take care of each other from now on, Pierrot," said Ernst from the front seat. "I need another man around the place. The way these women bully me is monstrous."

"But you're old," said Pierrot.

"I'm not *that* old."

"Twenty-seven is ancient."

"If he's ancient," asked Beatrix, "what does that make me?"

Pierrot hesitated for a moment. "Prehistoric," he said, giggling, and Beatrix burst out laughing.

"Oh my, little Pierrot," said Ernst. "You have a lot to learn about women."

"Did you have a lot of friends in Paris?" Beatrix asked, and Pierrot nodded.

"Quite a few," he said. "And one mortal enemy who called me *Le Petit* because I'm so small."

"You'll grow," said Beatrix, and "Bullies are everywhere," said Ernst at the same time.

"But my *very* best friend, Anshel, lived downstairs from us, and he's the one I miss the most. He's taking care of my dog, D'Artagnan, because I wasn't allowed to take him to the orphanage. I stayed with him for a few weeks when Maman died, but his mother didn't want me to live with them."

"Why not?" asked Ernst.

Pierrot thought about this and considered recounting the conversation he had overheard between Madame Bronstein and her friend in the kitchen that day, but decided against it. He still remembered how angry she had grown when she found him wearing Anshel's yarmulke and how she didn't want him to come to temple with them.

"Anshel and I spent most of our time together," he said, ignoring Ernst's question. "When he wasn't writing his stories, that is."

"His stories?" asked Ernst.

"He wants to be a writer when he grows up."

Beatrix smiled for a moment. "Is that what you want to be, too?" she asked.

"No," said Pierrot. "I tried a few times, but I could never get the words down sensibly. I used to make things up, though, or talk about funny things that happened at school, and then he would go away for an hour, and when he came back he'd hand me the pages. He always said that even though he had written it, it was still my story."

Beatrix's fingers drummed on the leather seats as she considered this. "Anshel . . . ," she said after a moment. "It was his mother who wrote to me, of course, and who told me where I could find you. Remind me, Pierrot, what was your friend's surname?"

"Bronstein."

"Anshel Bronstein. I see."

Once again Pierrot noticed his aunt's eyes flicker toward Ernst's in the rearview mirror, and this time the chauffeur offered a slight shake of his head, his expression quite serious now.

"It's going to be boring here," said Pierrot in a defeated tone.

"There's always plenty to do to keep you busy when you're not at school," said Beatrix. "And I'm sure we will find some work for you to do."

"Work?" asked Pierrot, looking at her in surprise.

"Yes, of course. Everyone in the house at the top of the mountain must work. Even you. Work will set us free—that's what the master says."

"I thought I was already free," said Pierrot.

"I thought that, too," said Ernst. "Turns out we were both wrong."

"Stop it, Ernst," snapped Beatrix.

"What kind of work?" asked Pierrot.

"I'm not sure yet," she replied. "The master might have some ideas on that subject. If not, I'm sure Herta and I will come up with something. Or you might help Emma in the kitchen. Oh, don't look so worried, Pierrot. These days, every German is obliged to contribute something to the Fatherland, no matter how young or how old."

"But I'm not German," said Pierrot. "I'm French."

Beatrix turned to him quickly, and the smile faded from her face. "You were born in France, that's true," she said. "And your mother was French. But your father, my older brother, was German. And that makes you German, too, do you understand? From now on, it's best that you don't even refer to where you came from."

"But why?"

"Because it will be safer that way," she said. "And there's one other thing I wanted to discuss with you. Your name."

"My name?" Pierrot asked, looking across at her and frowning.

"Yes." She hesitated, as if she could scarcely believe what she was about to say. "I don't think we should call you Pierrot anymore."

His mouth dropped open in surprise; he couldn't quite believe what she was saying. "But I've *always* been called Pierrot," he said. "It's . . . well, it's my name!"

"But it's such a *French* name. I thought perhaps we might call you Pieter instead. It's the same name, only the German version. It's not so very different."

"But I'm not a Pieter," insisted Pierrot. "I'm a Pierrot."

"Please, Pieter—"

"Pierrot!"

"Can you trust me on this? In your heart you can still be Pierrot, of course. But at the top of the mountain, when other people are around—and particularly when the master and the mistress are around—you will be Pieter."

Pierrot sighed. "But I don't like it," he said.

"You must understand that I only have your best interests at heart. That's why I brought you here to live with me. I want to keep you safe. And this is the only way I knew how to do it. I need you to be obedient, Pieter, even if it seems at times that the things I ask you to do are a little odd."

They drove on in silence for a while longer, still descending the mountain, and Pierrot wondered how much more his life was going to change before the year was out.

"What's the name of the town we're going to?" he asked finally.

"Berchtesgaden," replied Beatrix. "It's not too far now. We'll be there in a few minutes."

"Are we still in Salzburg?" Pierrot asked, for that was the last place name that had been tagged to his coat.

"No, we're about twenty miles from there," she replied. "The mountains you see around you are the Bavarian Alps. Over there"—she pointed out the left-hand window—"is the border with Austria. And over there"—she pointed out the right—"is Munich. You passed through Munich on the way here, didn't you?"

"Yes," said Pierrot. "And Mannheim," he added, remembering the soldier in the station who had stood on his fingers and seemed to enjoy the pain he was inflicting. "So over there," he added, reaching his hand out and pointing into the distance, over the mountains and into the unseen world beyond, "must be Paris. Over there is my home."

Beatrix shook her head and pressed Pierrot's hand back down. "No, Pieter," she said, looking back up toward the top of the mountain. "Up there is your home. On the Obersalzberg. That's where you live now. You mustn't think of Paris anymore. You may not see it again for a long time."

Pierrot felt a great sorrow building inside him, and Maman's face appeared in his mind, an image forming of them sitting side by side by the fireplace in the evening, while she carried on with her knitting and he read a book or did a bit of drawing in a sketchbook. He thought of D'Artagnan, and Madame Bronstein downstairs, and when he thought of Anshel, his fingers made the sign of the fox and then the sign of the dog.

I want to go home, he thought, twisting his hands in ways that only Anshel would understand.

"What are you doing?" asked Beatrix.

"Nothing," said Pierrot, placing his hands by his sides again and staring out the window.

A few minutes later they arrived in the market town of Berchtesgaden, and Ernst pulled the car into a quiet spot.

"Will you be long?" he asked, turning around and looking at Beatrix.

"A little while, perhaps," she said. "He needs clothes, he needs shoes. He could do with a haircut, too, don't you think? We need to make him a little less French and a little more German."

The chauffeur glanced at Pierrot for a moment and nodded. "Yes, probably," he said. "The smarter he looks, the better for all of us. He could still change his mind after all."

"Who could change his mind?" asked Pierrot.

"Shall we say two hours?" said Aunt Beatrix, ignoring him.

"Yes, that's fine."

"What time are you—?"

"Just before noon. The meeting will only take an hour or so."

"What meeting are you going to?" asked Pierrot.

"I'm not going to any meeting," replied Ernst.

"But you just said—"

"Pieter, shush," said Beatrix irritably. "Did no one ever tell you not to listen to other people's conversations?"

"But I'm sitting right here!" he protested. "How could I *not* hear you?"

"It's fine," said Ernst, turning to look at the boy and smiling. "Did you enjoy the drive?" he asked.

"I suppose so," said Pierrot.

"I expect one day you would like to learn to drive a car like this?"

Pierrot nodded. "I would," he said. "I like cars."

"Well, if you're good, then perhaps I will teach you. That will be a favor that I do for you. And in return, will you do a favor for me?"

Pierrot turned to look at his aunt, but she was silent.

"I can try," he said.

"No, I need you to do more than try," said Ernst. "I need you to promise."

"All right, I promise," agreed Pierrot. "What is it?"

"Your friend, Anshel Bronstein."

"What about him?" Pierrot asked, frowning.

"Ernst . . . ," said Beatrix nervously, leaning forward.

"Just a moment please, Beatrix," said the chauffeur

in the most serious tone he had used that morning. "The favor is that I want you never to mention this boy's name when you are in the house at the top of the mountain. Do you understand?"

Pierrot stared at him as if he had gone mad. "But why not?" he asked. "He's my best friend. I've known him since I was born. He's practically my brother."

"No," said the chauffeur in a sharp tone. "He's not your brother. Don't say such a thing. Think it, if you must. But don't say it out loud."

"Ernst is right," said Beatrix. "It will be for the best if you don't talk about your past at all. Keep your memories in your head, of course, but don't speak of them."

"And don't speak of this boy Anshel," insisted Ernst.

"I can't talk about my friends, I can't use my own name," said Pierrot in frustration. "Is there anything else that I can't do?"

"No, that's all," said Ernst, smiling at him. "You follow those rules, and one day I'll teach you to drive."

"All right," Pierrot said slowly, wondering whether the chauffeur was perhaps a little funny in the head— not a good attribute in a man who had to drive a car up and down a steep mountainside several times a day.

"Two hours, then," said Ernst as they got out.

As Pierrot walked away, he glanced back to see the chauffeur touch his aunt affectionately on the elbow, and they looked directly into each other's eyes, not smiling so much as sharing an anxious moment.

The market town was rather busy, and Aunt Beatrix said hello to a few acquaintances as they walked along, introducing Pierrot to them and telling them that he had come to live with her. There were a lot of soldiers there. Four were sitting outside a tavern, smoking and drinking beer, even though it was still early in the day. When they saw Beatrix approaching, they threw their cigarettes away and sat up straight. One tried to place his helmet in front of his beer glass, but it was far too tall to be hidden. Pierrot's aunt deliberately didn't look in their direction as she passed, but the boy couldn't help but be intrigued by the flurry of activity her arrival had provoked.

"Do you know those soldiers?" he asked.

"No," said Beatrix. "But they know me. They're worried that I will report them for drinking when they should be on patrol. Whenever the master is away, they become less conscientious in their duties. Now, here we are," she said as they arrived outside a clothes shop. "Don't these look suitable?"

The next couple of hours were perhaps the most boring of Pierrot's life. Beatrix insisted on his trying on traditional German boys' clothes—white shirts and lederhosen, held up by brown leather suspenders, with long kneesocks worn outside his trousers—and then he was taken to a shoe shop, where his feet were measured and he was forced to walk up and down the shop while everyone watched him. Afterward they returned to the first shop, where alterations had been made, and he had to try everything on all over again, one by one, and turn around in the center of the floor as his aunt and the assistant told him how handsome he looked.

He felt like an idiot.

"Can we go now?" he asked as his aunt paid the bill.

"Yes, of course," she replied. "Are you hungry? Should we get some lunch?"

Pierrot didn't need to think about this. He was always hungry, and when he told her this, Beatrix laughed out loud.

"Just like your father," she told him.

"Can I ask you something?" he asked as they entered a café and ordered soup and sandwiches. His aunt nodded.

"Yes, of course."

"Why didn't you ever come to see us when I was little?"

Beatrix considered this but waited until the food had arrived before speaking. "Your father and I, we were never very close as children," she said. "He was older than I was and we had little in common. But when he went to fight in the Great War, I missed him terribly and worried about him all the time. He wrote letters home, of course, and sometimes they made sense but sometimes they were rather incoherent. He was badly injured, as you know."

"No," said Pierrot, surprised. "No, I didn't know."

"Oh yes. I wonder why no one ever told you. He was in the trenches one night when a group of British soldiers attacked and overpowered them. They killed almost everyone, but somehow your father managed to escape—although he took a bullet to his shoulder that would have killed him had it been a few inches to the right. He hid in the forest nearby and watched as the soldiers dragged one unfortunate young boy from his hiding place—the last surviving soldier from that trench—and argued over what to do with him before one of the English simply shot him in the head. Somehow Wilhelm made it back to the German lines, but he'd lost a lot of blood and was delirious. They managed to patch him up and send him to the hospital for a few weeks, and he could have stayed—but no, he insisted on returning to the front when he was better." She looked around to make sure that she was not being overheard, and lowered her voice, almost to a whisper. "I think that his injuries, coupled with what he saw that night, did great damage to his mind. After the war, he was never the same. He grew so angry, so full of hatred toward anyone he thought had cost Germany her victory. We fell out over it. I hated to see how blinkered he was, and he claimed that I didn't know what I was talking about since I had never seen any of the action."

Pierrot frowned, trying to understand what she meant. "But weren't you on the same side?" he asked.

"Well, in a way," she replied. "But, Pieter, this isn't a conversation for now. Perhaps when you're older I'll be able to explain it better to you. When you understand a little more of the world. Now we need to eat quickly and get back. Ernst will be waiting for us."

"But his meeting won't be over yet."

Beatrix turned and stared at the boy. "He didn't have any meeting, Pieter," she said, her tone growing a little angry now, the first time he had heard her speak like this. "He is waiting in the same spot where we left him and he will be there when we return. Do you understand me?"

Pierrot nodded, a little frightened. "All right," he said, deciding not to bring the subject up again even though he knew what he had heard and there was no one in the world who could tell him anything different.

Chapter

7

The Sound That Nightmares Make

One Saturday morning a few weeks later, Pierrot woke to find the house in an uproar. The senior maid, Ute, was changing the linen on the beds and opening all the windows to let air into the rooms, while Herta was rushing around, her face even redder than usual, sweeping the floors and bringing out the mop and bucket to wash them clean.

"You'll have to fix your own breakfast today, Pieter," said Emma, the cook, when he went into the kitchen. There were baking dishes everywhere, and the delivery-man from Berchtesgaden must have already made his way to the top of the mountain, for crates of fresh fruit and vegetables were spread across all the work surfaces. "There's so much to be done and not a lot of time to do it in."

"Do you need any help?" he asked, because this was

one of those mornings when he'd woken up feeling rather lonely and couldn't face the idea of sitting around doing nothing all day.

"I need a lot of help," she replied, "but from a trained professional, not a seven-year-old boy. Perhaps later on there'll be something you can do for me. In the meantime, here"—she took an apple from one of the boxes and tossed it to him—"take this outside with you. It'll keep you going for a while."

He made his way back into the hallway, where Aunt Beatrix was standing with a clipboard in her hand, running her finger down a list and ticking things off as she went.

"What's going on?" he asked. "Why is everyone so busy today?"

"The master and the mistress are arriving in a few hours," she replied. "We received a telegram from Munich late last night, and it caught us all unawares. It's probably for the best if you just stay out of the way for now. Have you had a bath?"

"I had one last night."

"All right. Well, why don't you take a book and sit under one of the trees. It's a beautiful spring morning, after all. Oh, by the way . . ." She lifted the pages of her clipboard and extracted an envelope, holding it out to Pierrot.

"What's that?" he asked, surprised.

"It's a letter," she said, her tone growing stern.

"A letter for me?"

"Yes."

Pierrot stared at it in surprise. He couldn't think who might have written it.

"It's from your friend Anshel," said Beatrix.

"How do you know?"

"I opened it, of course."

Pierrot frowned. "You opened my letter?" he asked.

"And a good thing that I did," said Beatrix. "Believe me when I tell you that I am only looking out for your best interests."

He reached forward to take it, and, sure enough, the envelope had been sliced open at the top and its contents taken out and examined.

"You need to write back," continued Beatrix. "Today, preferably. And tell him never to write to you again."

Pierrot looked up at her in amazement. "But why would I do that?" he asked.

"I know it must seem strange," she replied. "But letters from this . . . this Anshel boy could get you into more trouble than you realize. You *and* me. It wouldn't matter if his name was Franz or Heinrich or Martin. But Anshel?" She shook her head. "A letter from a Jewish boy would not go down well here."

A huge argument erupted just before noon as Pierrot was kicking a ball around the garden. Beatrix came out to find Ute and Herta sitting on a bench at the rear of the house, smoking cigarettes and gossiping as they watched him.

"Look at the two of you just sitting there," she said angrily, "when the mirrors haven't been polished, the fireplace in the living room is filthy, and no one has brought the good rugs down from the attic yet."

"We were just taking a break," said Herta with a sigh. "We can't work every minute of the day, you know."

"You don't! Emma said you've been out here sunning yourselves for half an hour."

"Emma is a sneak," said Ute, folding her arms defiantly and staring off in the direction of the mountains.

"We could tell you things about Emma," added Herta. "Such as where the extra eggs go and how bars of chocolate keep going missing from the pantry. Not to mention what she gets up to with Lothar the milkman."

"I'm not interested in tittle-tattle," said Beatrix. "I just need to make sure everything gets done before the master arrives. Honestly, the way you girls carry on, sometimes I feel as if I'm in charge of a kindergarten."

"Well, you're the one who brought a child into the house, not us," snapped Herta, and there was a long silence as Beatrix stared at her furiously.

Pierrot came over, intrigued to see who would get the better of this exchange, but when his aunt saw him standing there, she pointed toward the house.

"Go inside, Pieter," she said. "Your room needs tidying."

"All right," he said, turning the corner out of sight but staying to overhear the rest of the conversation.

"Now, what did you just say?" Beatrix asked, turning back to Herta.

"Nothing," said Herta, looking down at her feet.

"Do you have any idea what that boy has been through?" she asked. "First his father leaves and is killed beneath the wheels of a train. Then his mother dies of tuberculosis and the poor boy is sent to an orphanage. And has he caused even a moment of trouble since his arrival here? No! Has he been anything but friendly and polite, despite the fact that he must still be grieving? No! Really, Herta, I would have hoped for a little more compassion from you. It's not as if you've had the easiest life, either, is it? You should understand what he's going through."

"I'm sorry," muttered Herta.

"Speak up."

"I said I'm sorry," said Herta, a little louder.

"She's sorry," echoed Ute.

Beatrix nodded. "All right," she said, her tone growing a little more conciliatory. "Well, let's have no more of these nasty comments—and certainly no more idleness. You wouldn't want the master to hear about any of this, would you?"

111

Both girls jumped up in fright when she said that and stamped their cigarettes out beneath their shoes before smoothing down their aprons.

"I'll polish the mirrors," said Herta.

"And I'll clean the fireplace," said Ute.

"Fine," said Beatrix. "I'll see to the rugs myself. Now, hurry up—they'll be here soon, and I want everything to be perfect."

As she walked back toward the house, Pierrot ran inside and reached for the broom in the hallway to take to his room.

"Pieter, dear," said Beatrix. "Be a darling and fetch my cardigan from my wardrobe, will you?"

"All right," he said, leaning the broom back against the wall as he made his way to the end of the corridor. He had only been in his aunt's room once before, when she gave him a tour of the house during his first week, and it had not been particularly interesting, containing much the same things as his own—a bed, a wardrobe, a chest of drawers, a jug and bowl—although it was the biggest by far of the staff rooms.

Opening the wardrobe, he retrieved the cardigan, but before leaving he noticed something he had not seen on his first visit. Hanging on the wall was a framed photograph of his mother and father, arm in arm, holding a small baby wrapped in blankets. Émilie was smiling widely, but Wilhelm looked downcast, and the baby—Pierrot himself, of course—was sound asleep. There was a date inscribed in the right-hand corner— *1929*—and the name of the photographer—*Matthias Reinhardt Photography, Montmartre*. Pierrot knew exactly where Montmartre was. He could remember standing on the steps of the Sacré-Cœur church while his mother told him how she had come there as a girl in 1919, just after the end of the Great War, to watch Cardinal Amette consecrate the basilica. She loved to wander through the flea markets, watching the artists as they painted on the streets; sometimes she, Wilhelm, and Pierrot would spend an entire afternoon just strolling around, eating snacks when they grew hungry, before making their way back home. It was a place where they had been happy as a family, when Papa was not as troubled as he would one day become, before Maman had fallen ill.

Leaving the room, Pierrot looked around for Beatrix, but she was nowhere to be seen, and when he roared out her name, she appeared quickly from the front parlor.

"Pieter," she cried. "Don't ever do that! There can be no running or shouting in this house. The master can't stand noise."

"Although he makes plenty of it himself," said Emma, stepping out of the kitchen, drying her wet hands on a tea towel. "Doesn't mind throwing a tantrum whenever he feels like it, does he? Shouts his bloody head off when things aren't going right."

Beatrix spun around and stared at the cook as if she had lost her mind. "One of these days that tongue of yours is going to get you into a lot of trouble," she said.

"You're not above me," replied Emma, pointing a finger at her. "So don't act as if you are. Cook and house-keeper are equal."

"I'm not trying to be above you, Emma," said Beatrix in an exhausted tone that suggested she had endured this conversation before. "I simply want you to realize how dangerous your words can be. Think whatever you want, but don't say such things out loud. Am I the only person in this house who has any sense?"

"I speak as I find," said Emma. "Always have done, always will do."

"Fine. Well, you speak like that to the master's face and see where it gets you."

Emma snorted, but it was obvious from the expression on her face that she would do no such thing. Pierrot began to worry about this master. Everyone seemed so afraid of him. And yet he'd been nice enough to allow Pierrot to come live there. It was all very confusing.

"Where's the boy?" asked Emma, looking around.

"I'm right here," said Pierrot.

"So you are. I can never find you when I want you. It's because you're so small. Don't you think it's about time you grew a little bigger?"

"Leave him alone, Emma," said Beatrix.

"I don't mean any harm. He reminds me of those little . . ." She tapped her forehead, trying to remember the word. "Who are those little fellows in that book?" she asked.

"What little fellows?" asked Beatrix. "What book?"

"You know!" insisted Emma. "The man arrives on the island and he's a giant compared to them, so they tie him up and—"

"Lilliputians," said Pierrot, interrupting her. "They're in *Gulliver's Travels*."

Both women stared at him in surprise. "How did you know that?" asked Beatrix.

"I've read it," he said with a shrug. "My friend Ansh—" He corrected himself. "The boy who lived downstairs from me in Paris had a copy. And there was one in the library in the orphanage, too."

"Stop showing off," said Emma. "Now, I told you that I might have a job for you later on, and I do. You're not squeamish, are you?"

Pierrot glanced toward his aunt, wondering whether he should go with her instead, but she simply took the cardigan from him and told him to follow Emma. As they walked through the kitchen, he breathed in the wonderful scent of baking that had been going on since early morning—a mixture of eggs and sugar and all types of fruit—and looked eagerly at the table, where tea towels were spread over the plates, concealing all their treasures.

"Eyes and hands off," said Emma, pointing at him. "If I come back in here and find anything missing, I'll know who to blame. I have everything counted, Pieter, and don't forget it." They stepped out into the back-yard and Pierrot looked around. "See them over there?" she asked, pointing at the chickens in the coop.

"Yes," said Pierrot.

"Have a look and tell me which two you think are the fattest."

Pierrot walked over and examined them carefully. There were more than a dozen gathered together, some standing still, some hiding behind others, and some pecking at the ground. "That one," he said, nodding at a chicken that was sitting down and looking about as unenthusiastic about life as a chicken possibly can. "And that one," he added, pointing at another, which was running around causing a great commotion.

"Right, then," said Emma, elbowing him out of the way and reaching forward to undo the lid of the coop. The chickens all started to squawk, but she reached in quickly and pulled out by their legs the two that Pierrot had chosen, standing up and holding them upside down, one in each hand.

"Close that," she said, nodding at the coop.

Pierrot did as he was told.

"Right. Now, follow me over here. The rest of them don't need to see what happens next."

Pierrot skipped around the corner after her, wondering what on earth she was going to do. This was quite easily the most interesting thing that had taken place in days. Perhaps they were going to play a game with the chickens or put them in a race to see which was the fastest.

"Hold this one," said Emma, handing the more subdued one to Pierrot, who took it reluctantly and held it by its feet as far away from his body as possible. It kept trying to turn its head to look at him, but he twisted and turned so it couldn't peck him.

"What happens now?" he asked, watching as Emma placed her chicken sideways on a sawed-off tree stump that came up to her waist, and held it firmly by the body.

"This," she said, reaching down with her other hand and picking up a hatchet, which she slammed down in a quick, efficient movement, slicing the chicken's head off before letting it fall to the ground. Decapitated, the body began running around in a frenzy, before slowing down and finally collapsing, dead, on the ground.

Pierrot stared in horror and felt the world begin to spin. He reached out to steady himself against the stump, but his hand landed in a pool of the dead chicken's blood, and he screamed, falling over and letting go of his own chicken—which, having witnessed its friend's unexpected end, made the sensible decision to run back toward the chicken coop as quickly as it could.

"Get up, Pieter," said Emma, marching past him. "If the master comes back and finds you lying out here like this, he'll have your guts for garters."

There was now an almighty cacophony coming from the coop, and the bird that was shut outside was panicking as it tried to get back in. The other chickens were looking at it and screeching, but of course there was nothing they could do. Before it knew what was happening, Emma was upon it, picking it up by the legs and carrying it over to the stump where, in an instant, it met the same grisly fate. Unable to look away, Pierrot felt his stomach begin to turn.

"If you throw up on that bird and ruin it," said Emma, waving the hatchet in the air, "you'll be next. Do you hear me?"

Pierrot stumbled to his feet and looked at the carnage around him—the two chicken heads lying in the grass, the spattered blood on Emma's apron—and ran back into the house, slamming the door shut. Even as he ran out of the kitchen and back to his room, he could hear Emma's laughter mixing with the noise of the birds until it all became one, the sound that nightmares make.

Pierrot spent most of the next hour lying on his bed, writing a letter to Anshel about what he'd just witnessed. Of course, he'd seen headless chickens hanging in the windows of the butchers' shops in Paris hundreds of times, and sometimes, when she had a little extra money, Maman would bring one home and sit by the kitchen table plucking the feathers from its body, telling him how they might get a week's worth of dinners from the bird if they were careful, but he had never actually witnessed one being killed before.

Of course, someone *has to kill them,* he reasoned with himself. But he didn't like the idea of cruelty. From as far back as he could recall, he had hated any sort of violence and instinctively walked away from confrontation. There were boys at school in Paris who would start fighting at the slightest provocation, who seemed to enjoy it; when two of them raised their fists and faced off against each other, the other children would gather in a circle around them, shielding them from the teachers and urging them on. But Pierrot never watched; he could never understand the enjoyment some people got from hurting others.

And that, he told Anshel, applied to chickens, too.

He didn't say much about the things Anshel had told him in his letter—how the streets of Paris were becoming more dangerous for a boy like him; how the bakery shop owned by Monsieur Goldblum had had its windows smashed and the word *Juden!* painted across its door; and how he had to step off the pavement and wait in the gutter if a non-Jew came along the street toward him. Pierrot ignored all this because it troubled

119

him to think of his friend being called names and bullied.

At the end of his letter, he told his friend that they should adopt a special code for writing to each other in the future.

We can't allow our correspondence to fall into enemy hands! So from now on, Anshel, we won't ever write our names at the end of our letters. Instead, we'll use the names we gave each other when we lived together in Paris. You must use the sign of the fox, and I will use the sign of the dog.

When Pierrot went back downstairs, he kept as far away from the kitchen as possible, not wanting to see what Emma might be doing to the dead birds. He could see his aunt brushing down the sofa cushions in the living room, where there was a wonderful view across the Obersalzberg. Two flags hung on the walls—long strips of fire-engine red with white circles in the center and four-hooked crosses within that were both impressive and scary. He walked on quietly, passing Ute and Herta, who were carrying trays of clean glasses into the main bedrooms, and then stopped at the end of the corridor, wondering what to do next.

The two doors to his left were closed, but he stepped into the library, making his way around the shelves, glancing at the titles of the books. It was a little disappointing, as none of them sounded as good as *Emil and the Detectives*; they were mostly history books and biographies of dead people. On one shelf there were a dozen copies of a single book—a book written by the master himself—and he flicked through one before replacing it on the shelf.

Finally he turned his attention to the table in the center of the room—a large rectangular desk with a map open on top of it, held down at its four corners by solid, smooth stones. He looked down and recognized the continent of Europe.

He leaned down, placing his index finger at the center of Europe, finding Salzburg quite easily but unable to locate the town, Berchtesgaden, that stood at the bottom of the mountain. He ran his finger westward across Zurich and Basel and into France until he reached Paris. He felt a great longing for home, for Maman and Papa, as he closed his eyes and recalled lying on the grass in the Champ de Mars with Anshel next to him and D'Artagnan running around, chasing unfamiliar smells.

So interested was he that he didn't hear the rush of people outside, the sound of the car pulling up the driveway, or Ernst's voice as he opened the doors to let the passengers out. Nor did he hear the welcomes extended and the sound of boots marching down the corridor toward him.

Only when he became aware that someone was

watching him did he turn around. A man was standing in the doorway: not very tall, but dressed in a heavy gray overcoat with a military cap under his arm, a small mustache sitting above his upper lip. He was staring at Pierrot as he removed his gloves slowly, methodically pulling on the fingers of each one. Pierrot's heart jumped; he recognized him immediately from the portrait in his room.

The master.

He remembered the instructions that Aunt Beatrix had given him on dozens of occasions since his arrival and tried to follow them exactly. He stood up straight, snapped his feet together, and clicked his heels once, quickly and loudly. His right arm shot out in the air, five fingers pointing directly ahead, just above the height of his shoulder. Finally he shouted, in the clearest, most confident voice that he could muster, the two words that he had practiced over and over since his arrival at the Berghof.

"Heil Hitler!"

Part

2

1937–1941

Chapter

8

The Brown Paper Package

Pierrot had been living at the Berghof for almost a year when the Führer gave him a present.

He was eight years old by now and enjoying life at the top of the Obersalzberg—even the strict daily routines that were set in place for him. Every morning, he rose at seven o'clock and ran outside to the storeroom to collect the bag of feed for the chickens—a mixture of grains and seeds—before pouring it into the trough for the birds' breakfast. Afterward, he would make his way to the kitchen, where Emma would prepare a bowl of fruit and cereal for him before he took a quick cold bath.

Ernst drove him to Berchtesgaden five mornings a week for school, and as he was the newest arrival and still spoke with a slight French accent, some of the children made fun of him, although the girl who sat next to him, Katarina, never did.

"Don't let them bully you, Pieter," she told him. "There's nothing I hate more than bullies. They're just cowards, that's all. You have to stand up to them whenever you can."

"But they're everywhere," replied Pierrot, telling her about the Parisian boy who had called him *Le Petit* and about the way Hugo had treated him in the Durand sisters' orphanage.

"So you just laugh at them," insisted Katarina. "You let their words fall off you like water."

Pierrot waited a few moments before saying what was really on his mind. "Don't you ever think," he asked cautiously, "that it would be *better* to be a bully than to be bullied? At least that way no one could ever hurt you."

Katarina turned to him in amazement. "No," she said definitively, shaking her head. "No, Pieter, I never think that. Not for a moment."

"No," he replied quickly, looking away. "No, neither do I."

In the late afternoons, he was free to run around the mountain to his heart's content, and as the weather was usually good at that altitude—bright and crisp with the fresh aroma of pine needles in the air—there was rarely a day when he didn't spend time outdoors. He climbed trees and headed off into the forest, venturing far from the house before finding his way back again using only his tracks, the sky, and his knowledge of the landscape for guidance.

He didn't think of Maman as much as he once had, although his father occasionally appeared in his dreams, always in uniform and usually with a rifle slung over his shoulder. He had also become less diligent in responding to Anshel, who now signed all his letters to the Berghof using the symbol that Pierrot had suggested—the sign of the fox—instead of his name. As every day passed and he hadn't written, he felt guilty for letting his friend down, but when he read Anshel's letters and heard about the things that were going on in Paris, he found that he simply couldn't think of anything to say.

The Führer was not present on the Obersalzberg very often, but whenever he was due to arrive, there was a great deal of panic and a lot of work that needed to be done. Ute had disappeared one night without even saying good-bye and was replaced by Wilhelmina, a silly girl who giggled constantly and would run into a different room whenever the master approached. Pierrot observed Hitler staring at her occasionally, and Emma, who had been cooking at the Berghof since 1924, thought she knew the reason why.

"When I first came here, Pieter," she told him over

breakfast one morning, closing the door and keeping her voice low, "this house wasn't called the Berghof at all. No, the master came up with that name. Originally it was called Haus Wachenfeld and it was a holiday home for a couple from Hamburg, the Winters. When Herr Winter died, however, his widow began renting it out to vacationers. That was terrible for me, because every time someone new came, I had to find out what kind of food they liked and how they wanted it cooked. I remember when Herr Hitler first came to stay in 1928 with Angela and Geli—"

"Who?" asked Pierrot.

"His sister and his niece. Angela once held the job that your aunt holds now. They came that summer, and Herr Hitler—he was Herr Hitler then, of course, not the Führer—informed me that he didn't eat meat. I had never heard of such a thing and thought it terribly odd. But over time I learned how to cook the dishes he preferred, and thankfully he didn't stop the rest of us from eating what we liked."

Almost on cue, Pierrot heard the sound of the chickens squawking in the backyard, as if they wished the Führer would impose his dietary standards on everyone.

"Angela was a tough woman," said Emma, sitting down and looking out the window as she cast her mind back nine years. "She and the master argued all the time, and it always seemed to be about Geli, Angela's daughter."

"Was she my age?" asked Pierrot, picturing a young girl running around the mountaintop every day as he did, which made him think that it might be a good idea to invite Katarina up there someday.

"No, much older," said Emma. "Around twenty, I think. She was very close to the master for a time. Too close, perhaps."

"How do you mean?"

Emma hesitated for a moment and shook her head. "It doesn't matter," she said. "I shouldn't be talking about these things. Especially not to you."

"But why not?" asked Pierrot, his interest growing now. "Please, Emma. I promise I won't tell anyone."

The cook sighed, and Pierrot could see that she desperately wanted to gossip. "All right," she said finally. "But if you breathe a word of what I'm about to tell you—"

"I won't," he said quickly.

"The thing is, Pieter, at this time the master was already leader of the National Socialist Party, which was gaining more and more seats in the Reichstag. He was building an army of supporters, and Geli enjoyed the attention he paid her. Until, that is, she grew bored of it. But if she was losing interest in him, the master still adored her and followed her everywhere. And then she fell in love with Emil, the Führer's driver at the time, and there was so much trouble over it. Poor Emil was dismissed from the master's service—he was lucky to escape with his life—Geli was inconsolable and Angela was furious, but the Führer wouldn't let her go. He insisted that Geli accompany him everywhere, and she, poor child, grew more and more withdrawn and unhappy. I think the Führer watches Wilhelmina so closely because she reminds him of Geli. They have a similar appearance. A big, round face. The same dark eyes and dimpled cheeks. Equally featherbrained. Really, Pieter, the first day she arrived, I thought I was seeing a ghost."

Pierrot considered all this while Emma returned to her cooking. After washing up his bowl and spoon, however, and replacing them in the cupboard, he turned to ask one last question.

"A ghost?" he said. "Why? What happened to her?"

Emma sighed and shook her head. "She went to Munich," she said. "He took her there. He refused to allow her out of his sight. And one day, when he left her alone in his apartment on the Prinzregentenplatz, she went into his bedroom, took a gun from his drawer, and shot herself through the heart."

Eva Braun almost always accompanied the Führer when he came to the Berghof, and Pierrot was under strict instructions to call her "Fräulein" at all times, even though they were not married. She was a tall lady in her early twenties with blond hair and blue eyes, and always dressed very fashionably. Pierrot had never seen her wear the same clothes twice.

"You can clear all this stuff out," she once told Beatrix when she was departing from the Obersalzberg after a weekend stay, throwing open her wardrobes and running a hand over all the blouses and dresses that hung there. "They're last season's fashions. The designers in Berlin have promised to send samples of their new collections directly."

"Shall I give them to the poor?" asked Beatrix, but Eva shook her head.

"It would be inappropriate," she said, "for any German woman, wealthy or impoverished, to wear a dress that had previously touched my skin. No, you can just throw them in the incinerator out back with all the other garbage. They're no good to me now. Just let them burn, Beatrix."

Eva did not pay very much attention to Pierrot—certainly nowhere near as much as the Führer did—but occasionally, when she passed him in a corridor, she would tousle his hair or tickle him under the chin, as if he were a spaniel, and say things like "Sweet little Pieter" or "Aren't you angelic?"—comments that embarrassed him. He didn't like being spoken down to and knew that she remained uncertain whether he worked for them, was an unwelcome tenant, or was simply a pet.

On the afternoon when he received the Führer's present, Pierrot was in the garden, not far from the main house, throwing a stick for Blondi, Hitler's German shepherd.

"Pieter!" cried Beatrix, stepping outside and waving to her nephew. "Pieter, come here, please!"

"I'm playing!" Pierrot shouted back, picking up the stick that Blondi had just retrieved for him and throwing it again.

"*Now*, Pieter!" insisted Beatrix, and the boy groaned as he made his way toward her. "You and that dog," she said. "Whenever I need you, all I have to do is follow the sound of barking."

"Blondi loves it up here," said Pierrot, grinning. "Do you think I should ask the Führer whether he might leave her here all the time from now on instead of taking her to Berlin with him?"

"I wouldn't if I were you," said Beatrix, shaking her head. "You know how attached he is to his dog."

"But Blondi loves it on the mountain. And from what I've heard, when she's at party headquarters, she's stuck inside meeting rooms and never gets out to play. You can see how excited she is whenever the car arrives and she jumps out."

"Please don't ask him," said Beatrix. "We don't ask the Führer for favors."

"But it's not for me!" insisted Pierrot. "It's for Blondi. The Führer won't mind. I think if *I* say it to him—"

"You've grown close, haven't you?" asked Beatrix, an anxious note creeping into her tone.

"Me and Blondi?"

"You and Herr Hitler."

"Shouldn't you call him the Führer?" asked Pierrot.

"Of course. I meant that. But it's true, isn't it? You spend a lot of time with him when he's here."

Pierrot thought about it, and his eyes opened wide when he realized why. "He reminds me of Papa," he told her. "The way he talks about Germany. About its destiny and its past. The pride he takes in his people. That's the way Papa used to talk, too."

"But the master's not your papa," said Beatrix.

"No, he's not," admitted Pierrot. "He doesn't stay up all night drinking, after all. Instead, he spends his time working. For the good of others. For the future of the Fatherland."

Beatrix stared at him and shook her head before looking away, her eyes glancing toward the tops of the mountains, and Pierrot thought that she must have got a sudden chill, for, quite unexpectedly, she shivered and wrapped her arms around herself.

"Anyway," he said, wondering whether he could go back and play with Blondi now. "Did you need me for something?"

"No," replied Beatrix. "He does."

"The Führer?"

"Yes."

"But you should have said," Pierrot cried, rushing past her toward the house, filled with anxiety that he might be in trouble. "You know he should never be kept waiting!"

He made his way quickly down the hallway toward the master's office, almost colliding with Eva as she emerged from one of the side rooms. Her arms flew out and she grabbed him by the shoulders, her fingers digging in so deeply that he squirmed.

"Pieter," she snapped. "Haven't I asked you not to run in the house?"

"The Führer wants to see me," said Pierrot quickly, struggling to release himself from her grasp.

"Did he ask for you?"

"Yes."

"Very well," she said, glancing up at the clock on the wall. "But don't keep him too long, all right? Dinner will be served soon, and I want to play some new records for him before we eat tonight. Music always helps with his digestion."

Pierrot skipped past her and knocked on the large

oak door, waiting until a voice inside beckoned him to enter. Closing the door behind him, he marched directly to the desk, clicked his heels together as he had done a thousand times over the last twelve months, and offered the one-armed salute that made him feel so important.

"Heil Hitler!" he roared at the top of his voice.

"Ah, there you are, Pieter," said the Führer, replacing the cap on his fountain pen and coming around the desk to look at him. "At last."

"I'm sorry, mein Führer," said Pierrot. "I got delayed."

"How so?"

He hesitated for a moment. "Oh, someone was talking to me outside, that's all."

"Someone? Who?"

Pierrot opened his mouth, the words on the tip of his tongue, but he felt anxious about saying them. He didn't want to get his aunt into trouble, but then again, it *was* her fault, he told himself, for not delivering the message more quickly.

"It doesn't matter," said Hitler after a moment. "You're here now. Sit down, please."

Pierrot sat on the edge of the sofa, perfectly straight, while the Führer sat opposite him in an armchair. A scratching sound came from outside the door, and Hitler glanced toward it. "You can let her in," he said, and Pierrot jumped up and opened the door. Blondi trotted inside, looking around for her master and coming to lie at his feet with an exhausted yawn. "Good girl," he said, reaching down to pat her. "You were having fun outside?" he asked.

"Yes, mein Führer," said Pierrot.

"What were you playing?"

"Fetch, mein Führer."

"You're very good with her, Pieter. I seem to be unable to train her. I can never discipline her. That's the problem. I am far too softhearted."

"She's very intelligent, so it's not difficult," said Pierrot.

"She belongs to an intelligent breed," replied Hitler. "Her mother was a smart dog, too. Did you ever have a dog, Pieter?"

"Yes, mein Führer," said Pierrot. "D'Artagnan."

Hitler smiled. "Of course," he said. "One of Dumas's three musketeers."

"No, mein Führer," said Pierrot.

"No?"

"No, mein Führer," he repeated. "The three musketeers were Athos, Porthos, and Aramis. D'Artagnan was just . . . Well, he was just one of their friends. Although he had the same job."

Hitler smiled. "How do you know all this?" he asked.

"My mother liked the book very much," he replied. "She named him when he was a puppy."

"And what breed was he?"

"I'm not sure," replied Pierrot, frowning. "A little bit of everything, I think."

The Führer made a disgusted face. "I prefer pure breeds," he said. "Do you know"—he almost laughed at the absurdity of the idea—"that one of the townspeople in Berchtesgaden once asked me whether I might allow his mongrel to sire pups from Blondi. His request was as audacious as it was repugnant. I would never allow a dog like Blondi to sully her bloodline by frolicking with such worthless creatures. Where is your dog now?"

Pierrot opened his mouth to tell the story of how D'Artagnan had gone to live with Madame Bronstein and Anshel after Maman's death, but remembered Beatrix's and Ernst's warnings that he should never mention his friend's name in the master's presence.

"He died," said Pierrot, looking at the floor and hoping that the lie would not be obvious on his face. He hated the idea of the Führer catching him in an untruth and losing his trust in him.

"I adore dogs," continued Hitler, offering no condolences. "My favorite was a little black-and-white Jack Russell who deserted from the English army during the war and came over to the German side."

Pierrot glanced up with a skeptical expression on his face; the idea of a canine deserter seemed unlikely to him, but the Führer smiled and wagged his finger.

"You think I'm joking, Pieter, but I assure you that

I am not. My little Jack Russell—I called him Fuchsl, or Little Fox—was a mascot for the English. They liked to keep small dogs in their trenches, you see, which was cruel of them. Some were used as messenger dogs; others as mortar detectors, for a dog can hear the sound of incoming shells much faster than a human can. Dogs have saved many a life in this way. Just as they can smell chlorine or mustard gas and alert their masters. Anyway, little Fuchsl went running out into no-man's-land one night—this must have been . . . oh, let me think . . . 1915, I suppose—and made his way safely through the artillery fire before leaping like an acrobat into the trench where I was stationed. Can you believe it? And from the moment he fell into my arms, he never left my side again for the next two years. He was more loyal and steadfast than any human I have ever known."

Pierrot tried to imagine the little dog charging across the terrain, dodging bullets, his paws slip-sliding on the blown-off limbs and ripped-out organs of the two armies. He'd heard these stories before from his father, and the idea made him feel queasy. "And what happened to him?" he asked.

The Führer's face grew dark. "He was taken from me in a despicable act of thievery," he replied in a low voice. "In August 1917, at a train station just outside Leipzig, a railway worker offered me two hundred marks for Fuchsl, and I said that I would never sell him, not for a thousand times that amount. But I used the bathroom before the train pulled out, and when I returned to my seat, Fuchsl, my little fox, was gone. Stolen!" The Führer breathed heavily through his nose, his lip curling, his voice rising in fury. It was twenty years later, but it was clear that he was still angered by the theft. "Do you know what I would do if I ever caught up with the man who stole my little Fuchsl?" he asked.

Pierrot shook his head, and the Führer leaned forward, indicating that the boy should lean forward, too. When he did, he held a hand up and whispered into his ear—three sentences, all quite short and very precise. When he was finished, he sat back, and something resembling a smile crossed his face. Pierrot sat back, too, but said nothing. He looked down at Blondi, who opened one eye and glanced upward without moving a muscle. As much as Pierrot liked spending time with the Führer, who always made him feel so important, at this moment he wanted nothing more than to be outside again with Blondi, throwing a stick into the forest, running as fast as he could. For fun. For the stick. For his life.

"But enough of this," said the Führer, patting the side of his armchair three times to signal that he wanted to change the subject. "I have a present for you."

"Thank you, mein Führer," said Pierrot, surprised.

"It's something that every boy your age should have." He pointed to a table next to his desk, where a brown paper package was sitting. "Fetch that for me, Pieter, will you?"

Blondi lifted her head at the word *fetch*, and the Führer laughed, patting the dog's head and telling her to rest easy. Pierrot walked over and collected the package, which held something soft inside, and carried it carefully over with both hands before holding it out for the master.

"No, no," said Hitler. "I already know what's inside. It's for you, Pieter. Open it. I think you'll like what you find there."

Pierrot's fingers started to undo the string that held the package together. It had been a long time since he'd received a present, and it was rather exciting to get one now.

"This is very kind of you," he said.

"Just open it," replied the Führer.

The strings came loose, the brown paper parted, and Pierrot reached inside to remove what lay there: a pair of black shorts, a light brown shirt, some shoes, a dark blue tunic, a black neckerchief, and a soft brown cap. A patch featuring a white bolt of lightning against a black background was sewn onto the left shirtsleeve.

Pierrot stared at the package's contents with a mixture of anxiety and desire. He remembered the boys on the train wearing clothes similar to this, with different designs but equal authority, how they had bullied him, and how Rottenführer Kotler had stolen his sandwiches. He wasn't sure that this was the type of person he wanted to be. But then again, those boys had been afraid of nothing and were part of a gang—just like the musketeers themselves, he thought. Pierrot quite liked the idea of being afraid of nothing. And he also liked the idea of belonging to something.

"These are very special clothes indeed," said the Führer. "You have heard of the Hitlerjugend, of course?"

"Yes," said Pierrot. "When I took the train to the Obersalzberg, I met some of them in a railway carriage."

"Then you know a little about them," replied Hitler. "Our National Socialist Party is making great strides in advancing the cause of our country. It is my destiny to lead Germany to great things around the world, and these, I promise you, will come in time. But it is never too early to join the cause. I am always impressed by how boys your age and a little older cleave to my side in support of our policies and our determination to right the wrongs that have been done in the past. You know what I am talking about, I presume?"

"A little," said Pierrot. "My father used to talk of such things."

"Good," said the Führer. "So we encourage our youth to join the party as soon as possible. We begin with the *Deutsches Jungvolk*. You're a little young, in truth, but I am making a special exception for you. In time, when you are older, you will become a member of the Hitlerjugend. There's a branch for girls, too, the *Bund Deutscher Mädel*—for do not underestimate the importance of the women who will be the mothers of our future leaders. Put your uniform on, Pieter. Let me see what you look like in it."

Pierrot blinked and looked down at the set of clothes. "Now, mein Führer?"

"Yes, why not? Go to your room and change. Come back here when you're fully dressed."

Pierrot went upstairs to his bedroom, where he took off his shoes, trousers, shirt, and sweater and replaced them with the clothes he had been given. They were a perfect fit. He put the shoes on last and clicked his heels together, impressed: They made a much more impressive sound than his own ever had. There was a mirror on the wall, and when he turned to look at his reflection, any anxiety that he might have felt immediately vanished. He had never felt so proud in all his life. He thought of Kotler again and realized how wonderful it would be to have such authority—to be able to take what you wanted, when you wanted, from whomever you wanted, instead of always having things taken from you.

When he returned to the Führer's study, Pierrot was wearing a broad grin on his face. "Thank you, mein Führer," he said.

"You are most welcome," replied Hitler. "But remember, the boy who wears this uniform must obey our rules and seek nothing more from life than the advancement of our party and our country. That is why we are here, all of us. To make Germany great again. And now there is one more thing." He walked over to his desk and shuffled through some papers until he found a card with some words written upon it. "Stand over here," he said, pointing toward the long Nazi banner that hung against one wall, a draping of red with the familiar white circle and hooked cross inscribed at its heart. "Now, take this card and read aloud what it says."

Pierrot stood where he was told and read the words slowly to himself first before looking up at the Führer nervously. He felt the most curious sensation inside. He wanted to speak the words aloud, and yet at the same time he did not want to speak them aloud.

"Pieter," said Hitler quietly.

Pierrot cleared his throat and stood tall. "In the presence of this blood banner," he began, "which represents our Führer, I swear to devote all my energies and my strength to the savior of our country, Adolf Hitler. I am willing and ready to give up my life for him, so help me God."

The Führer smiled, nodding, and took the card back, and as he did so, Pierrot hoped he did not notice how his small hands were trembling.

"Well done, Pieter," said Hitler. "From now on I don't want to see you wearing anything except this uniform, do you understand? You will find three further sets in your wardrobe."

Pierrot nodded and gave the salute once more before leaving the office and making his way down the corridor, feeling more confident and grown-up now that he was wearing a uniform. He was a member of the *Deutsches Jungvolk* now, he told himself. And not just any member, either. An important one, for how many other boys had been given a uniform by Adolf Hitler himself?

Papa would be so proud of me, he thought.

Turning a corner, he saw Beatrix and the chauffeur, Ernst, standing in an alcove together, talking quietly. He caught only a little of their conversation.

"Not quite yet," Ernst was saying. "But soon. If things get too far out of hand, I promise that I will act."

"And you know what you will do?" asked Beatrix.

"Yes," he replied. "I've spoken to—"

He stopped talking the moment he saw the boy.

"Pieter," he said.

"Look!" cried Pierrot, extending his arms wide. "Look at me!"

Beatrix said nothing for a moment but finally forced a smile onto her face. "You look wonderful," she said. "A true patriot. A true German."

Pierrot grinned and turned to look at Ernst, who was not smiling.

"And there was me thinking that you were French," Ernst said, touching the tip of his cap in Beatrix's direction before stepping through the front door and disappearing into the bright afternoon sunshine, a shadow dissolving into the white-and-green landscape.

Chapter

9

A Shoemaker, a Soldier, and a King

By the time Pierrot was eight years old, the Führer had grown closer to him and was showing an interest in what the boy was reading, allowing him full access to his library and recommending authors and books that impressed him. He presented Pierrot with a biography of an eighteenth-century Prussian king, Frederick the Great, written by Thomas Carlyle; a volume so enormous and with such a small typeface that Pierrot doubted whether he would even be able to get past the first chapter.

"A great warrior," explained Hitler, tapping the book's jacket with his index finger. "A global visionary. And a patron of the arts. The perfect journey: We fight to achieve our goals, we purify the world, and then we make it beautiful again."

Pierrot even read the Führer's own book, *Mein Kampf,*

which was a little easier for him to comprehend than the Carlyle but still confusing. He was particularly interested in the sections relating to the Great War, for that, of course, was where his father, Wilhelm, had suffered so much. Walking Blondi one afternoon in the forest surrounding the mountain retreat, he asked the Führer about his own time as a soldier.

"At first, I was a dispatch runner on the Western Front," he told him, "passing messages between the armies stationed at the French and Belgian borders. But then I fought in the trenches at Ypres, in the Somme, and at Passchendaele. Toward the end of the war, I was almost blinded in a mustard gas attack. Afterward, I sometimes thought that it would have been better to go blind than witness the indignities that the German people were made to suffer after their capitulation."

"My father fought in the Somme," said Pierrot. "My mother always said that although he didn't die in the war, it was the war that killed him."

The Führer brushed this comment away with a dismissive wave of his hand. "Your mother sounds like an ignorant person," he said. "Everyone should be proud to die for the greater glory of the Fatherland. Your father's memory, Pieter, is one that you should honor."

"But when he came home," said Pierrot, "he was very ill. And he did some terrible things."

"Such as?"

Pierrot didn't like to remember what his father had done, and when he began recounting some of the worst moments, he spoke quietly and looked down at the ground. The Führer listened without changing his expression, and when the boy finished, he simply shook his head, as if none of that mattered. "We will reclaim what is ours," he said. "Our land, our dignity, and our destiny. The struggle of the German people and our ultimate victory is the story that will define our generation."

Pierrot nodded. He had stopped thinking of himself as French and, becoming taller at last and having recently received two new *Deutsches Jungvolk* uniforms to accommodate his growing limbs, had begun to identify himself as German. After all, as the Führer told him, one day all of Europe would belong to Germany anyway, so national identities would no longer matter. "We will be one," he said. "United under a common flag." And with this, he pointed at the swastika armband that he wore. "That flag."

During that visit, the Führer gave Pierrot one more book from his private library before leaving for Berlin. Pierrot read the title carefully out loud. "*The International Jew*," he said, sounding out each syllable carefully. "*The World's Foremost Problem*. By Henry Ford."

"An American, of course," explained Hitler. "But he understands the nature of the Jew, the avarice of the Jew, the manner in which the Jew concerns himself with the accumulation of personal wealth. In my opinion, Mr. Ford should stop making cars and run for president. He is a man with whom Germany could work. With whom *I* could work."

Pierrot took the book and tried not to think about the fact that Anshel was Jewish but displayed none of the characteristics the Führer had described. For now, he put it in the drawer of the locker by his bed and returned to *Emil and the Detectives*, which always reminded him of home.

A few months later, as the autumn frost began to settle on the mountains and hills of the Obersalzberg, Ernst drove to Salzburg to collect Fräulein Braun, who was coming to the Berghof to prepare for the arrival of some very important guests. Emma was given a list of their favorite dishes, and she shook her head in disbelief.

"Well, they're not fussy at all, are they?" she said sarcastically.

"They're accustomed to certain standards," said Eva, who was already upset over the number of arrangements that had to be made; she walked around clicking her fingers at everyone and insisting that they work faster. "The Führer says that they are to be treated like . . . well, like royalty."

"I thought our interest in royalty ended with Kaiser Wilhelm," muttered Emma under her breath, before sitting down to compose a list of ingredients she would need to order from the farms around Berchtesgaden.

"I'm glad I'm at school today," Pierrot told Katarina between classes that morning. "Everyone is so busy at home. Herta and Ange—"

"Who's Ange?" asked Katarina, who was given a daily report of events at the Berghof by her friend.

"The new maid," explained Pierrot.

"Another maid?" she asked, shaking her head. "How many does he need?"

Pierrot frowned. He liked Katarina very much but didn't approve of her occasional mockery of the Führer. "She's a replacement," he told her. "Fräulein Braun got rid of Wilhelmina."

"So who does the Führer chase around the Berghof now?"

"There was a lot of commotion in the house this morning," he continued, ignoring this comment. He regretted ever having told her the story of Hitler's niece and Emma's theory that the maid reminded him of that unfortunate girl. "Every book is being taken off the shelves and dusted, every light removed and polished, every sheet washed, dried, and pressed until it looks like new once again."

"Such a lot of drama," said Katarina, "for such silly people."

The Führer arrived the night before their guests were due and undertook a thorough inspection of the residence, congratulating them all on the work they had done, much to Eva's relief.

The next morning, Beatrix called Pierrot into her room to check that his *Deutsches Jungvolk* uniform met the master's standards.

"Perfect," she said, looking him up and down approvingly. "You're getting so tall that I was worried it might be too short for you again."

There was a knock on the door, and Ange poked her head in. "Excuse me, miss," she said, "but—"

Pierrot turned and clicked his fingers sharply at her, just as he had seen Eva do, and pointed toward the corridor. "Get out," he said. "My aunt and I are talking."

Ange's mouth fell open in surprise, and she stared at him for a moment before stepping back outside and closing the door quietly behind her.

"There's no need to speak to her like that, Pieter," said Aunt Beatrix, who had been equally taken aback by Pierrot's tone.

"Why not?" he asked. He felt a little surprised that he had acted so authoritatively, but he rather liked the feeling of importance it gave him. "We were talking. She interrupted."

"But it's rude."

Pierrot shook his head, dismissing the idea. "She's just a maid," he said. "And I am a member of the *Deutsches Jungvolk*. Look at my uniform, Aunt Beatrix! She must show me the same respect that she would any soldier or officer."

Beatrix stood up and walked over to the window, staring out toward the mountaintops and the white clouds passing by overhead. She placed both hands on the windowsill as if trying to steady herself in case she let her temper get the better of her.

"Perhaps you shouldn't spend so much time with the Führer from now on," she said finally, turning around to look at her nephew.

"But why not?"

"He's a very busy man."

"A busy man who says that he sees great potential in me," said Pierrot proudly. "Besides, we talk about interesting things. And he listens to me."

"*I* listen to you, Pieter," said Beatrix.

"That's different."

"Why?"

"You're just a woman. Necessary to the Reich, of course, but the business of Germany is best left to men like the Führer and me."

Beatrix allowed herself a rather bitter smile. "This is something you decided for yourself, is it?"

"No," said Pierrot, shaking his head hesitantly. It

didn't sound quite right to him now that he heard the words spoken out loud. After all, Maman had been a woman, and she had always known what was best for him. "It's what the Führer told me."

"And you're a man now, are you?" she asked. "At only eight years of age?"

"I'll be nine in a few weeks," he said, standing up to his full height. "And you said yourself that I'm getting taller by the day."

Beatrix sat down on the bed and patted the quilt, inviting him to sit next to her. "What kind of things does the Führer talk to you about?" she asked.

"It's rather complicated," he replied. "It has to do with history and politics, and the Führer says that the female brain—"

"Try me. I'll do my best to keep up."

"We talk about how we have been robbed," he said.

"*We*? Who is this *we*? You and I? You and him?"

"All of us. The German people."

"Of course. You're German now. I forgot."

"My father's birthright is my own," replied Pierrot defensively.

"And what have we been robbed of exactly?"

"Our land. Our pride. The Jews stole it from us. They're taking over the world, you see. After the Great War—"

"But, Pieter," she said, "you must remember that we lost the Great War."

"Please don't interrupt me when I'm speaking, Aunt Beatrix," said Pierrot with a sigh. "It shows a lack of respect on your part. Of course I remember that we lost, but you in turn must accept that we suffered indignities afterward that were designed to humiliate us. The Allies could not be content with victory. They wanted the German people on their knees as retribution. Our country was filled with cowards who gave in to our enemies too easily. We will not make that mistake again."

"And your father?" asked Beatrix, looking him directly in the eye. "Was he one of those cowards?"

"The worst of all. For he allowed weakness to vanquish his spirit. But I am not like him. I am strong. I will restore pride to the name of Fischer." He stopped and stared at his aunt. "What's the matter?" he asked. "Why are you crying?"

"I'm not crying."

"But you are."

"Oh, I don't know, Pieter," she said, looking away. "I'm just tired, that's all. The preparation that has gone into the arrival of our guests has been overwhelming. And sometimes I think . . ." She hesitated, as if apprehensive about finishing this sentence.

"You think what?"

"That I made a terrible mistake in bringing you here. I thought I was doing the right thing. I thought that by keeping you close I could protect you. But as every day goes past—"

Another knock on the door, and when it opened, Pierrot spun around angrily, but this time he did not snap his fingers, for it was Fräulein Braun who was standing there. He jumped off the bed and stood to attention while Aunt Beatrix remained exactly where she was.

"They're here," Fräulein Braun said in an excited voice.

"What do I call them?" whispered Pierrot as, filled with excitement and trepidation, he took his place in the receiving line next to his aunt.

"Your Royal Highness," she said. "To both of them. The duke and the duchess. But don't say anything at all unless they speak to you first."

A few moments later, a car turned the corner at the top of the driveway, and almost simultaneously the Führer appeared behind Pierrot, and the staff stood rigidly at attention, eyes facing forward. When Ernst pulled up and turned the ignition off, he jumped out quickly to open the rear door. A small man wearing a suit that looked a little tight on him stepped out clutching a hat. He glanced around, his expression one of confusion mixed with disappointment at the lack of fanfare that awaited him.

"One is generally accustomed to a band of some sort," he mumbled—more to himself than to anyone in particular—before offering a well-practiced Nazi salute, his arm shooting proudly into the air, as if he had been particularly looking forward to this moment.

"Herr Hitler," he said in a refined voice as he switched effortlessly from English to German. "So nice to meet you at last."

"Your Royal Highness," replied the Führer, smiling. "Your German is excellent."

"Yes, well," he muttered, fiddling with his hatband. "One's family, you know . . ." He trailed off, as if uncertain how to finish this sentence.

"David, aren't you going to introduce me?" asked a woman who had stepped out of the car behind him. She was dressed entirely in black, as if she were attending a funeral. Her broad American accent could be heard as she switched the conversation back to English.

"Oh yes, of course. Herr Hitler, may I present Her Royal Highness, the Duchess of Windsor."

The duchess pronounced herself charmed, as did the Führer, who also complimented her on her German.

"It's not quite as good as the duke's," she said, smiling. "But I get by."

Eva stepped forward to be introduced, standing firmly erect as she shook hands, apparently anxious not to be seen to be offering anything even close to a curtsy. The two couples made small talk for a few moments, speaking of the weather, the view from the Berghof, and the drive up the mountain.

"Thought we might go over the side a few times," remarked the duke. "One wouldn't want to have vertigo, would one?"

"Ernst would never have allowed any harm to come to you," replied the Führer, glancing over at the chauffeur. "He knows how important you are to us."

"Hmm?" asked the duke, looking up as if he'd only just realized that he was in the middle of a conversation. "What's that you say?"

"Let's go inside," replied the Führer. "You like to take tea at this hour, am I right?"

"A little whiskey, if you have it," said the duke. "The altitude, you know. It takes it out of one. Wallis, are you coming?"

"Yes, David. I was just admiring the house. Isn't it beautiful?"

"My sister and I found it in 1928," said Hitler. "We stayed here once on vacation, and I liked it so much that as soon as I could afford to, I bought it. I come here now whenever I can."

"It's important for men in our position to have a place of their own," said the duke, tugging at his shirt cuffs now. "Somewhere the world will leave us alone."

"Men in our position?" asked the Führer, raising an eyebrow.

"Important men," said the duke. "I had such a place back in England, you know. When I was Prince of Wales. Fort Belvedere. Wonderful getaway. We threw some extraordinary parties in those days, didn't we, Wallis? I tried to lock myself away there and throw away the key, but somehow the prime minister always got in."

"Perhaps we can find a way for you to return the favor," said the Führer, smiling broadly. "Come, let's get you that drink."

"But who is this little fellow?" asked the duchess as she passed Pierrot. "Isn't he dressed beautifully, David? He's like a wonderful little Nazi toy. Oh, I'd like to take him home with me and put him on the mantelpiece, he's so precious. What's your name, sunshine?"

Pierrot looked up at the Führer, who nodded.

"Pieter, Your Royal Highness," said Pierrot.

"The nephew of our housekeeper," explained Hitler. "The poor boy was orphaned, so I agreed that he should come live here."

"You see, David?" said Wallis, turning to her husband. "That's what I call real honest-to-goodness Christian charity. This is what people don't understand about you, Adolf. Now, I can call you Adolf, can't I? And you must call me Wallis. They don't see that underneath all these uniforms and military lah-di-dah there lies the heart and soul of a true gentleman. And as for you, Ernie," she said, turning to the chauffeur and wagging a gloved finger in his direction, "I hope now you see that—"

"Mein Führer," said Beatrix, stepping forward quickly, her voice surprisingly loud as she cut the duchess off. "Would you like me to organize drinks for your guests?"

Hitler glanced at her in surprise but, amused by what the duchess had been saying, simply nodded. "Of course," he said. "But inside, I think. It's getting chilly out here."

"Yes, there was talk of whiskey, wasn't there?" said the duke, marching in, and as the hosts and the staff followed, Pierrot glanced around and was surprised to see that Ernst was leaning against the car, his face quite pale, paler than he'd ever seen him before.

"You've gone quite white," said Pierrot, before mimicking the duke's accent. "The altitude, you know. It takes it out of one, doesn't it, Ernst?"

Later that evening Emma handed Pierrot a tray of pastries and asked him to take them into the study, where the Führer and the duke were deep in conversation.

"Ah, Pieter," said the Führer as he came in, tapping the table between the two armchairs. "You can lay that down here."

"Can I get you anything else, mein Führer? Your Royal

Highness?" he asked, but he was so anxious that he addressed each man by the other's title, which made them both laugh.

"That'd be a thing, wouldn't it?" said the duke. "If I came over here to run Germany?"

"Or if I took over England," replied the Führer.

The duke's smile faded a little at these words, and he fiddled with his wedding ring, pulling it on and off nervously.

"Do you always have a boy doing these jobs, Herr Hitler?" he asked. "Don't you have a valet?"

"No," said the Führer. "Do I need one?"

"Every gentleman does. Or at least a footman in the corner of the room in case you require anything."

Hitler considered this and shook his head, as if he could not quite understand the other man's sense of protocol. "Pieter," he said, pointing toward the corner. "Stand over there in the corner. You can be an honorary footman during the duke's visit."

"Yes, mein Führer," said Pierrot proudly, moving over to a place beside the door and trying his best to breathe as quietly as possible.

"You've been awfully good to us," the duke continued, lighting a cigarette. "Everywhere we went, we were treated with such generosity of spirit. We're tremendously pleased." He leaned forward. "Wallis is right—I really do think that if the English people could get to

know you a little, then they would see what a jolly decent
fellow you are. You have a lot in common with us, you
know."

"Is that so?"

"Yes, we share a sense of purpose and a belief in the
important destiny of our people."

The Führer said nothing but leaned forward to pour
his guest another drink.

"The way I see it," the duke said, "our two countries
have much more to gain by working together than apart.
Not a formal alliance, of course, more a sort of *entente
cordiale* like what we have with the French, although one
can never be too trusting when it comes to them. No
one wants a repeat of the madness of twenty years ago.
Too many innocent young men lost their lives in that
conflict. On both sides."

"Yes," replied the Führer quietly. "I fought in it."

"As did I."

"You did?"

"Well, not in the trenches, of course. I was heir to the
throne then. I had a position. I still have a position, you
know."

"But not the one to which you were born," said the
Führer. "Although that could change, I suppose. In time."

The duke glanced around, as if worried that there
might be spies hiding behind the curtains. His eyes never
once landed on Pierrot; the boy might have been a statue

for all the interest he held for him. "You know that the British government didn't want me to come here," he said in a confidential tone. "And my brother Bertie was in agreement with them. There was an awful fuss. Baldwin, Churchill, all of them rattling their sabers."

"But why do you listen to them?" asked Hitler. "You're no longer king. You're a free man. You can do whatever you choose."

"I'll never be free," said the duke mournfully. "And anyway, there's the question of resources, if you follow me. One can't simply go out and get a job."

"But why not?"

"What would you have me do? Work behind the gentlemen's counter at Harrods? Open a haberdashery shop? Put myself out as a footman like our young friend over there?" He laughed as he pointed toward Pierrot.

"All honest jobs," said the Führer quietly. "But perhaps beneath your status as a former king. There are perhaps other . . . possibilities." The duke shook his head, ignoring the question completely, and the Führer smiled. "Do you ever regret your decision to abdicate the throne?"

"Not for a moment," replied the duke, and even Pierrot could hear the deceit in his voice. "Couldn't do it, you see. Not without the help and support of the woman I love. Said as much in my farewell speech. But they were never going to allow her to be queen."

"And you think that's the only reason they got rid of you?" asked the Führer.

"Don't you?"

"I think they were frightened of you," he said. "Just as they're frightened of me. They knew how closely connected you felt our countries should be. Why, your own great-grandmother Queen Victoria was the grandmother of our last Kaiser. And your great-grandfather Prince Albert was from Coburg. Your country is as invested in mine as mine is in yours. We are like a pair of great oak trees planted close together. Our roots are intertwined beneath the ground. Cut one down, and the other suffers. Allow one to flourish, and both will."

The duke considered this for a moment before replying. "There may be something in that," he said.

"You have been robbed of your birthright," continued the Führer, his voice raised now in anger. "How can you bear it?"

"Nothing a chap can do," said the duke. "It's all over and done with now."

"But who knows what the future might hold?"

"What do you mean?"

"Germany is going to change over the years to come. We grow strong once again. We are redefining our place in the world. And perhaps England will change, too. You're a forward-thinking man, I believe. Don't you think that the duchess and you could do more good for your people if you were reinstated as king and queen?"

The duke bit his lip and frowned. "Can't be done," he said after a moment. "I had my chance."

"Anything can be done. Look at me—I am the leader of a unified German people and I came from nothing. My father was a shoemaker."

"My father was a king."

"My father was a soldier," said Pierrot from the corner of the room, the words out of his mouth before he could take them back, and the two men turned to look at him as if they had forgotten that he was even present. The Führer threw the boy a look of such fury that he felt his stomach lunge inside and thought he might be sick.

"All things are possible," continued the Führer after a moment as the two men turned back to face each other. "If it could be done, would you take back your throne?"

The duke looked around anxiously and bit his nails, examining each one in turn before wiping his hand on his pants leg. "Well, of course one has to consider one's duty," he replied. "And what might be best for one's country. Any way that one could serve, naturally one would . . . one would . . ."

He looked up hopefully, like a puppy hoping to be taken into the care of a benevolent master, and the Führer smiled. "I think we understand each other,

David," he said. "You don't mind me calling you David, do you?"

"Well, it's just that no one does, you see. Other than Wallis. And my family. Although they don't call me anything anymore. I never hear from them. I phone Bertie four or five times a day, but he won't take my calls."

The Führer held up his hands. "Forgive me," he said. "We shall stick with the formalities. Your Royal Highness." He shook his head. "Or perhaps one day, once again, Your Majesty."

Pierrot emerged slowly from a dream, feeling as if he had only been asleep for a couple of hours. His half-open eyes registered the darkness of the room and the sound of breathing. Someone was standing over him, staring down at him as he slept. He opened his eyes completely now to see the face of the Führer, Adolf Hitler, and his heart leaped in fright. He tried to sit up to salute, but as he did so, he found himself being pushed back down onto the bed. He had never seen the master with such an expression on his face before. It was even more frightening than the one he had seen when he interrupted his conversation with the duke earlier.

"Your father was a soldier, was he?" hissed the Führer. "Better than mine? Better than the duke's? You think because he's dead that he was braver than me?"

"No, mein Führer," said Pierrot breathlessly, the words

catching in his throat. His mouth felt terribly dry, and his heart was pounding fiercely in his chest.

"I can trust you, Pieter, can't I?" asked the Führer, leaning over so the bristles of his mustache were almost touching the boy's upper lip. "You will never give me cause to regret allowing you to live here?"

"No, mein Führer. Never, I promise it."

"You'd better not," he hissed. "Because disloyalty never goes unpunished."

He tapped Pierrot twice on the cheek before marching out of the room, closing the door behind him.

Pierrot lifted the sheets and looked down at his pajamas. He felt like crying; he had done something that he hadn't done since he was a baby, and he didn't know how he was going to explain it to anyone. But he swore one thing to himself: He would never let the Führer down again.

Chapter

10

A Happy Christmas
at the Berghof

The war had been going on for more than a year, and life at the Berghof had changed considerably. The Führer was spending less time on the Obersalzberg, and when he was there, he was usually locked away in his office with his most senior generals, the leaders of the Gestapo, the Schutzstaffel, and the Wehrmacht. Although Hitler still made time to talk to Pierrot on his visits, the officers who ran these divisions of the Reich—Göring, Himmler, Goebbels, and Heydrich—preferred to ignore him completely. He longed for the day when he might hold such an exalted position as theirs.

Pierrot no longer slept in the small bedroom that had been his since arriving on the mountain. Once he turned eleven, Hitler informed Beatrix that the boy was to take her room and that she should move her things into the smaller one—a decision that made Emma shake her

head and mutter something about the boy's lack of gratitude toward his aunt.

"The decision was the Führer's," declared Pierrot, not
even bothering to look at her as he spoke. He had grown
taller—no one would call him *Le Petit* anymore—and his
chest had begun to grow muscular from the daily exercise he took across the mountaintops. "Or do you question his decisions? Is that it, Emma? Because if that is the
case, we could always discuss it with him?"

"What's going on here?" asked Beatrix, entering the
kitchen and sensing the strained atmosphere between
the two.

"Emma seems to think that we should not have
swapped bedrooms," said Pierrot.

"I said no such thing," muttered Emma, turning away.

"Liar," said Pierrot to her retreating back. Turning
around, he noticed the expression on his aunt's face and
felt a curious mixture of emotions. He wanted the bigger
room, of course, but he also wanted her to recognize that
it was his right to have it. After all, it was closer to the
Führer's own room. "You don't mind, do you?" he asked.

"Why should I mind?" asked Beatrix, shrugging
her shoulders. "It's just a place to sleep, that's all. It's not
important."

"It wasn't my idea, you know."

"Wasn't it? I heard differently."

"No! All I said to the Führer was that I wished my

bedroom had a wall large enough to hold one of the big European maps, that's all. Like yours. Then I could follow the progress of our army across the continent as we defeat our enemies."

Beatrix laughed, but it didn't sound to Pierrot like the type of laugh a person made when they found something funny.

"We can swap back if you like," he said quietly, looking down at the floor.

"It's fine," said Beatrix. "The move has been made. It would be a waste of all our time to put everything back as it once was."

"Good," he said, looking up again and smiling. "I knew you'd agree. Emma has an opinion on everything, doesn't she? If you ask me, servants should just keep their mouths shut and get on with their work."

One afternoon Pierrot made his way to the library in search of something to read. Running his fingers across the spines of the books that lined the walls, he examined a history of Germany and another of the European continent, before considering a book that described all the crimes committed by the Jewish people throughout history. Next to it was a thesis denouncing the Treaty of Versailles as an act of criminal injustice against the Fatherland. He skipped past *Mein Kampf*, which he had read three times over the last eighteen months and from which he could quote many important paragraphs. Squeezed in at the end of one shelf was a final volume, and he smiled to remember how young and innocent he had been when Simone Durand had thrust it into his hands at the train station in Orléans four years earlier. *Emil and the Detectives.* How had it found its way into a bookcase filled with such important works? he wondered. Taking it out, he glanced toward Herta, who was on her knees sweeping out the fireplace. As he opened it, an envelope fell from the pages and he picked it up.

"Who's that from?" asked the maid, looking up at him.

"An old friend of mine," he said, his voice betraying his anxiety at seeing the familiar handwriting. "Well, just a neighbor really," he added, correcting himself. "No one important."

It was the last letter from Anshel that Pierrot had bothered to save. He opened it again now, however, and looked at the first few lines. There was no salutation, no "Dear Pierrot"; just a drawing of a dog and then some rushed sentences:

I'm writing this in haste as there is a lot of noise from the street outside and Maman says that the day to leave has finally arrived. She's packed some of our belongings, the most important things, and they've been in suitcases by the front door for weeks now. I'm not sure where we're going, but Maman says it's not

safe for us here anymore. Don't worry, Pierrot, we're
taking D'Artagnan with us! How are you, anyway?
Why haven't you replied to my last two letters?
Everything has changed here in Paris. I wish you could
see how

Pierrot didn't read any further but simply crumpled the letter up and tossed it in the fireplace, causing some of the previous night's ash to blow out into Herta's face.

"Pieter!" she snapped angrily, but he ignored her. He wondered whether he should have destroyed the letter in the kitchen fireplace instead, which had been roaring since early that morning. After all, if the Führer found it, he might be angry with him, and he could imagine nothing worse than suffering his disapproval. He had liked Anshel once—of course he had—but they were just children back then, and he hadn't understood what it meant to be friends with a Jew. It was for the best that he cut off their acquaintance. He reached back in and retrieved it, handing the book across to Herta as he did so.

"You may give this to a child in Berchtesgaden with my compliments," he instructed her imperiously. "Or simply throw it away. Whichever is easier."

"Oh, Erich Kästner," said Herta, smiling as she looked at the dust jacket. "I remember reading this when I was younger. Wonderful, isn't it?"

"It's for children," said Pierrot with a shrug,

determined not to agree with her. "Now, get back to work," he added, walking away. "I want this place clean before the Führer returns."

A few days before Christmas Pierrot woke in the middle of the night in need of the bathroom and made his way quietly down the corridor in his bare feet. Returning, still half asleep, he made the mistake of heading for his old room, only realizing his error as he reached for the door handle. He was about to turn away when, to his surprise, he heard voices inside. Curiosity got the better of him, and he leaned close to the woodwork to listen.

"But I'm afraid," Aunt Beatrix was saying from inside. "For you. For me. For all of us."

"There's nothing to fear," said the second voice, which Pierrot recognized as that of Ernst the chauffeur. "Everything is carefully planned. Remember, there are more people on our side than you might imagine."

"But is this really the best place? Would Berlin not be better?"

"There's too much security there, and he feels safe in this house. Trust me, my darling, nothing will go wrong. And when it's over, and wiser heads prevail, we can chart a new course. We are doing the right thing. You believe that, don't you?"

"You know I do," said Beatrix fiercely. "Every time I look at Pierrot, I know what needs to be done. He's already a completely different boy from the one who first came to live here. You've seen it, haven't you?"

"Of course I have. He's becoming one of them. He's getting more like them every day. He's even started ordering the servants around. I scolded him a few days ago, and he told me that I should take my complaints to the Führer or be silent."

"I dread to think what type of man he'll become if this continues," said Beatrix. "Something must be done. Not just for him but for all the Pierrots out there. The Führer will destroy the whole country if he's not stopped. The whole of Europe. He says that he is illuminating the minds of the German people—but no, he is the darkness at the center of the world."

There was silence for a few moments, and Pierrot could hear the unmistakable sound of his aunt and the chauffeur kissing. He was almost ready to open the door and confront them, but instead he went back to his own room and lay in bed with his eyes open, staring at the ceiling, repeating their conversation over and over in his mind as he tried to understand what it all might mean.

At school the next day he wondered whether he should discuss what was happening at the Berghof with Katarina, and he found her at lunchtime, reading a book beneath one of the great oak trees in the garden. They no longer sat together in class; Katarina had requested that she be moved next to Gretchen Baffril, the quietest girl in the school, but had never given Pierrot a reason why she didn't want to sit next to him anymore.

"You're not wearing your tie," said Pierrot, picking it up from where she had thrown it on the ground. Katarina had become a member of the *Bund Deutscher Mädel* a year earlier, and she was constantly complaining about being forced to wear the uniform.

"*You* wear it if it means that much to you," said Katarina, not looking up from her book.

"But I'm already wearing a tie," said Pierrot. "Look."

She glanced up at him for a moment before taking it from him. "I suppose if I don't put this on, then you'll tell on me," she asked.

"Of course not," he said. "Why would I do that? As long as you're wearing it again by the time lunch is over and classes have restarted, then it's not a problem."

"You're so fair-minded, Pieter," she said with a sweet smile. "That's one of the things I like about you."

Pierrot smiled back at her—though, to his surprise, she simply rolled her eyes and went back to her book. He considered leaving her alone, but he had a question that he wanted to ask and he couldn't think who else to approach. He didn't seem to have many friends in their class anymore.

"Do you know my aunt Beatrix?" he said finally, sitting down next to her.

"Yes, of course," said Katarina. "She comes into my father's shop all the time to buy paper and ink."

"And Ernst, the Führer's chauffeur?"

"I've never spoken to him, but I've seen him driving through Berchtesgaden. What about them?"

Pierrot breathed heavily through his nose and then shook his head. "Nothing," he said.

"How could it be nothing? You brought their names up."

"Do you think they are good Germans?" he asked her then. "No, that's not a sensible question. I suppose that would depend on how you define the word *good*, wouldn't it?"

"Not really," said Katarina, putting the bookmark in the center of her novel and looking directly at him. "I don't think there are too many ways to define the word *good*. You're either good or you aren't."

"I suppose I meant do you think that they're patriots?"

"How would I know?" asked Katarina, shrugging her shoulders. "Although there are, of course, different ways to define patriotism. You, for example, might have the opposite view of it from me."

"My view is the same as the Führer's view," said Pierrot.

"Well, exactly," said Katarina, looking away toward a group of children who were playing hopscotch in the corner of the yard.

"Why don't you like me as much as you used to?" he asked after a long silence, and she looked back at him, the expression on her face suggesting that she was surprised by his question.

"What makes you think I don't like you, Pieter?" she asked.

"You don't talk to me like you used to. And you moved seats to sit beside Gretchen Baffril and never told me why."

"Well, Gretchen had no one to sit next to," said Katarina, "after Heinrich Furst left the school. I didn't want her to be alone."

Pierrot looked away and swallowed hard, already regretting beginning this conversation.

"You remember Heinrich, don't you, Pieter?" she continued. "Such a nice boy. So friendly. You remember how we were all shocked when he told us the things his father had said about the Führer? And how we all promised to tell no one?"

Pierrot stood up and brushed down the seat of his trousers. "It's getting cold out here," he said. "I should go back inside."

"You remember how we heard that his father had been taken from his bed in the middle of the night and dragged out of Berchtesgaden and no one ever heard from him again? And how Heinrich and his mother and his

176

younger sister had to move to Leipzig to stay with her sister because they had no money anymore?"

A bell rang from the doorway of the school, and Pierrot glanced at his watch. "Your tie," he said, pointing at it. "It's time. You should put it on."

"Don't worry, I will," she said as he walked away. "After all, we wouldn't want poor Gretchen to be left sitting on her own again tomorrow, would we? Would we, *Pierrot*?" she shouted after him, but he was shaking his head, pretending that she wasn't speaking to him; and somehow, by the time he got back inside, he had removed their conversation from his memory and placed it in a different part of his mind—the part that housed the memories of Maman and Anshel, a place he rarely visited anymore.

The Führer and Eva arrived at the Berghof the day before Christmas Eve while Pierrot was outside practicing marching with a rifle, and after they had settled in, he was summoned indoors. "There's going to be a party in Berchtesgaden later today," explained Eva. "A Christmas party for the children. The Führer would like you to accompany us."

His heart jumped in excitement. He never went anywhere with the Führer, and he could only imagine the envious expressions on the faces of the townspeople when he arrived with their beloved leader. It was almost as if he was Hitler's son.

He put on a clean uniform and instructed Ange to shine his boots until she could see her reflection in them. When she brought them to him, Pierrot barely glanced at them before saying they were not good enough and sent her away to do them again.

"And don't make me ask a third time," he said as she made her way back to the maids' parlor.

When he stepped out onto the gravel with Hitler and Eva that afternoon, he felt more proud than he had ever been in his life. The three sat together in the backseat of the car, and as they made their way down the mountain, Pierrot watched Ernst in the rearview mirror, trying to decipher his intentions toward the Führer; but whenever the chauffeur glanced up to check the road behind him, he seemed oblivious to the boy's presence. *He thinks I'm just a child*, thought Pierrot. *He thinks I don't matter at all.*

When they arrived in Berchtesgaden, the crowds were out on the streets, waving their swastikas and cheering loudly. Despite the cold weather, Hitler had told Ernst to keep the top down so the people could see him, and they roared their approval as he drove by. He saluted them all, a stern expression on his face, while Eva smiled and waved. When Ernst came to a halt outside the town hall, the mayor emerged to greet them, bowing obsequiously as the Führer shook his hand, then saluting, then bowing some more, then growing so confused that it was only when Hitler placed a hand on his shoulder to calm him that he moved out of the way to let them enter.

"Aren't you coming inside, Ernst?" asked Pierrot, noticing that the chauffeur was holding back.

"No, I must stay with the car," he said. "But you go in. I'll be here when you all come out again."

Pierrot nodded and decided to wait until the rest of the crowd had entered; he liked the idea of striding down the aisle in his *Deutsches Jungvolk* uniform and taking his seat next to the Führer with the eyes of the townspeople upon him—but just as he was about to go inside, he noticed Ernst's car keys lying on the ground next to his feet. The chauffeur must have dropped them in the rush of the crowd.

"Ernst," he cried, looking down the road toward where the car was parked. He sighed in frustration, glancing back toward the hall, but there were still so many people trying to find seats that he decided he had enough time, and ran down the road, expecting to see the chauffeur patting down his pockets as he searched for his keys.

The car was there, but to his surprise Ernst was nowhere to be seen.

Pierrot frowned and looked around. Hadn't Ernst said that he was going to stay with the car? He began to walk back, looking up and down the side streets, and just as he was about to give up and return to the town hall, he spotted the chauffeur knocking on a door up ahead.

"Ernst," he cried, but his voice didn't carry far enough, and as he watched, the door of a small, nondescript cottage opened and Ernst disappeared inside. Pierrot held back until the street was quiet again, then went up to the window and put his face to the glass.

There was no one in the front room, which was filled with books and records, but beyond the door, Pierrot saw Ernst standing with a man he had never seen before. They were deep in conversation, and Pierrot watched as the man opened a cupboard and removed what looked like a bottle of medicine and a syringe. He pierced the lid with the needle, extracted some of the liquid inside, and injected a cake that stood on the table next to him before spreading his arms wide, as if to say, *It's that simple*. Nodding, Ernst took the bottle and syringe and placed them in the pocket of his overcoat, while the man picked up the cake and threw it away. When the chauffeur turned to make his way back to the front door, Pierrot ran quickly around the corner but stayed close to hear whatever they might say.

"Good luck," said the stranger.

"Good luck to all of us," replied Ernst.

Pierrot made his way back toward the hall, stopping only to place the keys in the ignition of the car as he passed by, and took a seat near the front as he listened to the end of the Führer's speech. Hitler was saying that the next year, 1941, was going to be a great year for Germany; that the world would finally recognize their resolve as victory grew closer. Despite the festive atmosphere, he roared out his lines as if he were admonishing the audience, and they shouted back in delight, whipped into a frenzy by his almost manic enthusiasm. He banged the podium a few times, making Eva close her eyes and jump, and the more he banged, the more the crowd cheered and raised their arms in the air as one, as if they were a single body connected by a single mind, shouting *"Sieg Heil! Sieg Heil! Sieg Heil!"* with Pierrot at their heart, his voice as loud as anyone's, his passion as deep, his belief as strong.

On Christmas Eve the Führer hosted a small party for the staff at the Berghof, thanking them for their service throughout the year. Although he did not give any personal gifts, he had asked Pierrot a few days earlier whether there was anything special that he would like, but the boy, not wanting to seem like a child among adults, declined the offer.

Emma had excelled herself with a buffet feast consisting of turkey, duck, and goose, each filled with a wonderful spiced apple and cranberry stuffing; three types of potato; sauerkraut; and a range of vegetable dishes for the Führer. The group ate together cheerfully,

Hitler making his way from person to person, talking politics still, and no matter what he said, everyone nodded and told him that he was absolutely right. He might have said that the moon was made of cheese, and they would have said, *Of course it is, mein Führer. Limburger.*

Pierrot watched his aunt, who seemed more nervous than usual this evening, and kept a close eye on Ernst, who appeared remarkably calm.

"Take a drink, Ernst," said the Führer loudly, pouring a glass of wine for the driver. "Your services will not be required tonight. It's Christmas Eve, after all. Enjoy yourself."

"Thank you, mein Führer," said the chauffeur, accepting the glass and raising it in a toast to their leader, who accepted their applause with a polite nod and a rare smile.

"Oh, the pudding!" cried Emma when the plates on the table were almost empty. "I almost forgot the pudding!"

Pierrot watched as she carried in a beautiful stollen from the kitchen and placed it on the table, the scent of fruit, marzipan, and spices filling the air. She had done her best to fashion the cake into the shape of the Berghof itself, with icing sugar sprinkled liberally over the top to represent the snow, although it would have been a generous critic who complimented her skills as a sculptor. Beatrix stared at it, her face pale, and turned to look at

Ernst, who was resolutely not looking in her direction. Pierrot watched nervously as Emma took a knife from the pocket of her apron and began to slice it.

"It looks wonderful, Emma," said Eva, beaming in delight.

"The first slice for the Führer," said Beatrix, her voice raised but with a slight tremble to it.

"Yes, of course," agreed Ernst. "You must tell us if it is as good as it looks."

"Sadly, I don't think I can eat another thing," declared Hitler, patting his stomach. "I'm ready to burst as it is."

"Oh, but you must, mein Führer!" cried Ernst immediately. "I'm sorry," he said quickly, noticing everyone's look of surprise at his enthusiasm. "I only meant that you must reward yourself. You have done so much for us this year. One slice, please. To celebrate the festive season. And afterward, we can all enjoy some."

Emma cut a generous portion and put it on a plate with a small fork before handing it across, and the Führer looked at it for a moment uncertainly before laughing and accepting it.

"Of course you're right," he said. "It's not Christmas without stollen." He used the side of his fork to cut a section of the cake and brought it to his lips.

"Wait!" cried Pierrot, jumping forward. "Stop!"

All heads turned in astonishment as the boy ran over to the Führer's side.

"What is it, Pieter?" he asked. "Do *you* want the first slice? I thought you had more manners than that."

"Put the cake down," said Pierrot.

There was perfect silence for a few moments. "I beg your pardon?" said the Führer finally, his tone cold.

"Put the cake down, mein Führer," repeated Pierrot. "I don't think you should eat it."

No one said a word as Hitler stared from the boy to the cake and back to Pierrot again.

"Why ever not?" he asked, baffled.

"I think there might be something wrong with it," Pierrot said, his voice trembling as badly as his aunt's had a few moments before. Perhaps he was wrong in what he suspected. Perhaps he was making a fool of himself and the Führer would never forgive his outburst.

"Something wrong with my stollen?" cried Emma, breaking the silence. "I'll have you know, young man, that I've been making that cake for more than twenty years and have never received a word of complaint!"

"Pieter, you're tired," said Beatrix, stepping forward and placing her hands on his shoulders, trying to steer him away. "Forgive him, mein Führer. It's all the excitement of Christmas. You know what children are like."

"Get off me," shouted Pierrot, pulling away from her, and she stepped back, one hand pressed across her mouth in horror. "Don't you ever put your hands on me again, do you hear? You're a traitor!"

"Pieter," said the Führer. "What are you—?"

"You asked me earlier whether I would like anything for Christmas," he said, interrupting his master.

"I did, yes. What of it?"

"Well, I've changed my mind. I *do* want something. Something very simple."

The Führer looked around the room, a half smile on his face, as if he hoped that someone would explain all this to him soon. "All right," he said. "What is it? Tell me."

"I want Ernst to eat the first slice," he said.

No one spoke. No one moved. The Führer tapped his finger against the side of the plate as he considered this, before slowly, very slowly, turning to look at his driver.

"You want Ernst to eat the first slice," he repeated quietly.

"No, mein Führer," insisted the chauffeur, shaking his head, the words cracking as he said them. "I couldn't. It would be wrong. The honor of the first slice belongs to you. You have done . . ." His words started to trail off in fear. "So much . . . for us all . . ."

"But it's Christmas," said the Führer, walking toward him, and both Herta and Ange stepped out of the way to let him pass. "And young people should get what they want for Christmas, if they have been good. And Pieter has been very, very good."

He held out the plate, looking directly into Ernst's eyes. "Eat it," he said. "Eat it all. Tell me how good it tastes."

He took a step back as Ernst lifted the fork to his mouth, staring at it for a few moments before suddenly throwing the entire thing at the Führer and running from the room, the plate crashing to the floor and breaking as Eva let out a scream.

"Ernst!" cried Beatrix, but the guards ran after him quickly, and Pierrot could hear shouting from outside as they struggled with him before dragging him to the ground. He was shouting at them to leave him alone, to let him be, while Beatrix, Emma, and the maids watched in fear and shock.

"What is it?" asked Eva, staring around in confusion. "What's going on? Why wouldn't he eat it?"

"He has tried to poison me," said the Führer in a sad voice. "How very disappointing."

And with that, he turned away, walked down the corridor and into his office, and closed the door behind him. A moment later he opened it again and roared out Pierrot's name.

It took a long time for Pierrot to fall asleep that night, and not because he was excited about the arrival of

Christmas morning. Interrogated by the Führer for more than an hour, he had willingly revealed everything he had seen and heard since his arrival at the Berghof: the suspicions he had felt toward Ernst, and his great disappointment in his aunt for betraying the Fatherland in the way she had. Hitler remained silent throughout much of what the boy said, asking only a few questions from time to time, querying whether Emma, Herta, Ange, or any of his guards had been involved in the plan, but it seemed that they had been as ignorant of what Ernst and Beatrix had been planning as the Führer himself.

"And you, Pieter?" he asked before letting him go. "Why did you never think to bring your concerns to me before?"

"I didn't understand what they were doing until tonight," he replied, his face growing red with anxiety that he, too, would be implicated in what had happened and sent away from the Obersalzberg. "I wasn't even sure that it was you Ernst was talking about. I only realized at the last moment, when he insisted that you eat the stollen."

The Führer accepted this and sent him to bed, where he lay, tossing and turning, until sleep somehow overtook him. Fretful images of both his parents came to him in his dream: the chessboard downstairs in Monsieur Abrahams's restaurant; the streets around the Avenue Charles-Floquet. He dreamed of D'Artagnan and Anshel and the stories his friend used to send him. And then, just as his dreams became more confused, he woke with a start, sitting up in bed with perspiration running down his face.

He sat there, one hand pressed against his chest, struggling to get enough air into his lungs, and heard the sound of low voices and crunching boots outside on the gravel. Jumping out of bed, he went to the window and parted the curtains, looking out onto the gardens that were spread out toward the rear of the Berghof. The soldiers had brought two cars around—Ernst's and one other—and they were parked on opposite sides, headlights turned on, providing a ghostly spotlight in the center of the lawn. Three soldiers were standing with their backs to the house, and as Pierrot watched, he saw two more leading Ernst out to stand at the point where the beams of light intersected, giving him a rather ghostly appearance. His shirt had been ripped off and he had been badly beaten. One eye was sealed shut, and blood ran down his face from a deep wound at his hairline. A dark bruise had formed on his abdomen. His hands were tied behind his back, and although his legs threatened to give way beneath him, he stood tall, like a man.

A moment later, the Führer himself appeared, wearing his overcoat and hat, and stood to the right of the soldiers, saying not a word but simply nodding at them as they raised their rifles.

"Death to the Nazis!" cried Ernst as the bullets rang out, and Pierrot gripped the windowsill in horror as he saw the chauffeur's body fall to the ground; then one of the guards who had delivered him to his place of death marched over, took a pistol from his holster, and discharged a single bullet into the dead man's head. Hitler nodded once again, and they reached down, dragging Ernst's body away by his feet.

Pierrot pressed a hand to his mouth to prevent himself from screaming out loud and fell to the floor, his back against the wall. He had never seen anything like this before; he felt as if he might be sick.

You did this, said a voice in his head. *You killed him.*

"But he was a traitor," he said aloud in reply. "He betrayed the Fatherland! He betrayed the Führer himself!"

He stayed where he was, trying to compose himself, ignoring the perspiration that ran down his pajama top, and finally, when he felt strong enough, he stood up and dared to look outside.

Immediately he heard the crunching noise of the guards' footsteps once again, and then the sound of women's voices crying out hysterically. Looking down, he saw that Emma and Herta had emerged from the house and were standing next to the Führer, pleading with him, the former practically on her knees in an attitude of supplication, and Pierrot frowned, unable to understand what was happening now. Ernst was dead, after all. It was too late to plead for his life.

And then he saw her.

His aunt Beatrix was being led to the spot where Ernst himself had fallen a few minutes earlier.

Unlike the chauffeur's, her hands were not tied behind her back, but her face had been beaten just as badly and her blouse torn down the center. She didn't speak, but looked across at the women for a moment with a grateful expression before turning away. The Führer let out an almighty roar at the cook and the maid, and now Eva appeared, dragging the weeping women back inside the house.

Pierrot looked toward his aunt, and his blood froze as he saw that she was looking up at his window, staring directly at him. Their eyes met and he swallowed, uncertain what to do or say, but before he could decide, the shots rang out like an insult to the tranquillity of the mountains, and her body fell to the ground. Pierrot simply stared, unable to move. And then, once again, the sound of a single additional bullet cut through the night.

But you are safe, he told himself. *And she was a traitor, just like Ernst. Traitors must be punished.*

He closed his eyes as her body was dragged away, and when he finally opened them again, he expected the area to be empty—but there was one man left standing in the center of the garden, looking up at him just as Beatrix had a few moments before.

Pierrot stayed very still as his eyes met the eyes of Adolf Hitler. He knew what he had to do. Clicking his heels together, he shot his right arm forward, his finger-tips grazing the glass, and offered the salute that had become so much a part of him.

It was Pierrot who had climbed out of bed that morning, but it was Pieter who returned to it now before falling soundly asleep.

Part

3

1942–1945

Chapter

11

A Special Project

The meeting had been going on for almost an hour when two men finally arrived. Pieter watched from the study as Kempka, the new chauffeur, pulled up to the front door, and he ran outside quickly, ready to greet the officers as they stepped out of the car.

"Heil Hitler!" he shouted at the top of his voice, standing at attention as he saluted, and Herr Bischoff, the shorter, more portly of the pair, put a hand to his heart in surprise.

"Must he shout so loudly?" he asked, turning to the driver, who glanced toward the boy with a disdainful expression. "Who is he anyway?"

"My name is Scharführer Fischer," declared Pieter, tapping the gorget patches on his shoulders to indicate the two white lightning bolts set against a black background. "Kempka, bring the bags inside."

"Of course, sir," said the driver, acting upon the boy's words without hesitation.

The other man, an Obersturmbannführer by his insignia, whose right arm was in a cast, stepped forward and examined the insignia that Pieter wore before looking into the boy's eyes without even a hint of warmth or friendliness. There was something about his face that was familiar to Pieter but he couldn't quite place him. He was sure that he hadn't seen him at the Berghof before, as he kept a careful log of all the senior officers who visited, but somewhere at the back of his mind he felt certain that their paths had already crossed.

"Scharführer Fischer," said the man quietly. "You are a member of the Hitlerjugend?"

"Yes, mein Obersturmbannführer."

"And how old are you?"

"Thirteen, mein Obersturmbannführer. The Führer advanced me into my position a year ahead of other boys following a great service that I provided to him and to the Fatherland."

"I see. But surely a squadron leader needs a squad?"

"Yes, mein Obersturmbannführer," replied Pieter, looking straight ahead.

"So where is it?"

"Mein Obersturmbannführer?"

"Your squad. How many members of the Hitlerjugend are under your authority? A dozen? Twenty? Fifty?"

"There are no members of the Hitlerjugend present on the Obersalzberg," replied Pieter.

"None at all?"

"No, mein Obersturmbannführer," said Pieter, embarrassed. While he was proud of his designation, it was a source of shame to him that he had never trained, lived, or spent any time with other members of the organization, and although the Führer occasionally offered him a new title, a promotion of sorts, it was obvious that these were largely honorary.

"A squadron leader without a squad," said the man, turning around and smiling at Herr Bischoff. "I've never heard of such a thing."

Pieter felt his face grow red and wished that he had not come out here at all. They were jealous of him, that was all, he told himself. He would make them pay some day when real power was his.

"Karl! Ralf!" cried the Führer, emerging from the house and marching down the steps to shake the two men's hands. He was in uncommonly good humor. "At last—what kept you?"

"My apologies, mein Führer," said Kempka, the heels of his boots clicking together sharply as he saluted. "The train from Munich to Salzburg was delayed."

"Then why are you apologizing?" asked Hitler, who did not enjoy the same amicable relationship with his driver as he had with his predecessor—although, as Eva had pointed out one evening when he mentioned this, at least Kempka had never tried to kill him. "You didn't delay it, did you? Come in, gentlemen. Heinrich is inside. I'll be with you in a few minutes. Pieter will show you the way to my study."

The two officers followed the boy down the corridor, and when he opened the door to where Himmler was waiting, the Reichsführer forced himself to smile as he shook the men's hands. Pieter noticed that, although he was friendly toward Bischoff, he seemed a little more hostile toward his companion.

Leaving the men alone and making his way back through the house, he saw the Führer standing by one of the windows, reading a letter.

"Mein Führer," he said, walking up to him.

"What is it, Pieter? I'm busy," he replied, putting the letter in his pocket and looking at the boy.

"I hope I have proved my worth to you, mein Führer," said Pieter, standing at attention.

"Yes, of course you have. Why do you ask?"

"It's something that the Obersturmbannführer said. About my having a rank without any responsibilities."

"You have many responsibilities, Pieter. You're part of life here on the Obersalzberg. And you have your studies, of course."

"I thought that perhaps I could be of more assistance to you in our struggle."

"Assistance in what way?"

"I would like to fight. I'm strong, I'm healthy, I'm—"

"Thirteen," interrupted the Führer, a half smile crossing his face. "Pieter, you're only thirteen. And the army isn't a place for a child."

Pieter felt his face grow red with frustration. "I'm not a child, mein Führer," he said. "My father fought for the Fatherland. I wish to fight, too. To make you proud of me and to regain honor for my family name, which has been tarnished so badly."

The Führer breathed heavily through his nose as he considered this. "Do you ever wonder why I kept you on here?" he asked finally.

Pieter shook his head. "Mein Führer?" he asked.

"When that treasonous woman, whose name I shall not mention, asked me whether you could come to live with her at the Berghof, I was initially skeptical. I have no experience of children. As you know, I have none of my own. I wasn't sure that I wanted one running around here, getting under my feet. But I have always been soft-hearted, and so I acquiesced, and you have never made me regret my decision, for you proved to be a quiet, studious presence. After her crimes were discovered, there were many who said that you should be sent away or even meet the same fate."

Pieter's eyes opened wide. Someone had suggested that he be shot for the misadventures of Beatrix and

Ernst? Who had it been? One of the soldiers, perhaps? Herta or Ange? Emma? They hated his authority at the Berghof. Had they wanted him to die for it?

"But I said no," continued the Führer, clicking his fingers as Blondi passed; the dog came over and nuzzled his hand. "I said that Pieter is my friend, that Pieter looks after my welfare, that Pieter will never let me down. Despite his heritage. Despite his despicable family. Despite it all. I said that I would keep you here until you were a man. But you are not a man yet, little Pieter."

The boy blanched at the adjective, feeling the frustration build within him.

"When you are older, perhaps there will be something that we can do for you. But of course the war will be long over by then. We will achieve victory in the next year or so, that much is obvious. In the meantime, you must continue with your studies—that's what is most important. And a few years from now, there will be an important position waiting for you within the Reich. Of that I am sure."

Pieter nodded, disappointed, but he knew better than to question the Führer or try to persuade him to change his mind. He had seen on more than one occasion how quickly he could lose his temper and switch from benign to angry. He clicked his heels together, offered the traditional salute, and stepped back outside, where Kempka was standing against the car, smoking a cigarette.

"Stand up straight," he shouted. "Don't slouch."

And the driver immediately stood up straight.

And stopped slouching.

Alone in the kitchen, Pieter opened cookie jars and cupboards in search of something to eat. He was always hungry these days, and no matter how much he ate, he never seemed to be satisfied, which Herta said was typical of teenagers. Lifting the lid off a cake stand, he smiled when he saw a fresh chocolate cake waiting for him and was about to cut into it when Emma walked through the door.

"If you so much as touch that cake, Pieter Fischer, I'll have you over my knee with the wooden spoon before you know what's hit you."

Pieter turned around and stared at her coldly; he had been insulted enough for one day. "Don't you think I'm a little old for these threats of yours?" he asked.

"No, I don't," she said, pushing him out of the way and replacing the glass cloche over the cake. "When you're in my kitchen, you play by my rules. I don't care how important you think you are. If you're hungry, there's some leftover chicken in the fridge. You can make yourself a sandwich."

He opened the fridge door and glanced inside. Sure enough, a plate of chicken was sitting on one of the shelves, along with a bowl of stuffing and a fresh bowl of mayonnaise.

"Perfect," he said, clapping his hands together in delight. "That looks delicious. You can make it for me. I'll have something sweet afterward."

He sat down at the table, and Emma stared at him with her hands on her hips. "I'm not your bloody servant," she said. "If you want a sandwich, you can make it yourself. You have arms, don't you?"

"You're the cook," he said quietly. "And I am a hungry Scharführer. You will make me a sandwich." Emma didn't move, but he could see that she was uncertain how to respond. All it needed was a little persistence on his part. "Now!" he roared, slamming his fist down on the table, and she jumped to attention, muttering under her breath as she took the ingredients from the fridge and opened the bread bin to cut two thick slices. When it was ready and she placed it before him, he looked up and smiled.

"Thank you, Emma," he said calmly. "It looks delicious."

She held his gaze for a long time. "It must be a family trait," she said. "Your aunt Beatrix always loved a chicken sandwich, too. Although she knew how to make one herself."

Pieter set his jaw firmly and felt a fury build inside him. He didn't have an aunt Beatrix, he told himself. That was another boy entirely. A boy named Pierrot.

"By the way," she said, reaching into the pocket of her apron. "This arrived for you earlier."

She handed him an envelope, and he glanced at the familiar handwriting for a moment before giving it back to her, unopened.

"Burn it," he said. "And any others like it that I receive."

"It's from that old friend of yours in Paris, isn't it?" she asked, holding it up to the light as if she might be able to see right through the paper to the words inside.

"I said burn it," he snapped. "I *have* no friends in Paris. And certainly not this Jew who insists on writing to tell me how terrible his life is now. He should be glad that Paris has fallen to the Germans. He's lucky to be permitted to live there still."

"I remember when you first came here," said Emma quietly. "You sat over there, on that stool, and told me about little Anshel and how he was taking care of your dog for you, and how you and he had a special sign language that only you understood. He was the fox and you were the dog and—"

Pieter didn't allow her to finish her sentence, jumping off his seat and grabbing the envelope from her hands with such force that she slipped backward and fell to the floor. She cried out, even though she could not have hurt herself very badly.

"What's the matter with you?" he hissed. "Why must you always treat me with such disrespect? Don't you know who I am?"

"No," she cried, her voice filled with emotion. "No, I don't. But I know who you used to be."

Pieter felt his hands clench into fists, but before he could say anything more, the Führer opened the door and looked in.

"Pieter!" he said. "Come with me, will you? I need your assistance."

He glanced down at Emma but seemed indifferent to the fact that she was lying on the kitchen floor. Pieter threw the letter in the fire and looked down at the cook.

"I don't want to receive any more of these letters, do you understand me? If any come, throw them away. If you bring another one to me, I will make you regret it." He picked up the uneaten sandwich from the table and walked over to the garbage can, throwing it inside. "You can make me a fresh one later," he said. "I'll let you know when I require it."

"As you can see, Pieter," said the Führer when he stepped into the room, "the Obersturmbannführer here has injured himself. Some business with a thug on the street who attacked him."

"He broke my arm," remarked the man calmly, as if it barely mattered. "So I broke his neck."

Himmler and Herr Bischoff looked up from the table in the center of the room, which contained photographs and many pages of diagrams, and laughed.

"Anyway, he can't write for the time being, so he needs a note-taker. Sit down, stay quiet, and write down what we say. No interruptions."

"Of course, mein Führer," said Pieter, remembering how frightened he had been almost five years earlier when the Duke of Windsor had sat in this same room and he had spoken out of turn.

Pieter was reluctant at first to sit at the Führer's desk, but the four men were gathered around the table, so he had no choice. He sat down and pressed his hands flat against the wood, feeling an enormous sense of power as he glanced around the room, the flags of the German state and the Nazi party standing on either side of him. It was hard not to imagine what it would be like to sit here as the one in charge.

"Pieter, are you paying attention?" snapped Hitler, turning to look at him, and the boy sat up straight, pulled a notepad toward him, unscrewed a fountain pen from the desk, and began to write down what was said.

"Now, here, of course, is the proposed site," said Herr Bischoff, pointing down at a series of schematics. "As you know, mein Führer, the sixteen buildings that were here originally have been converted for our use, but there is simply not enough room there for the number of prisoners that are being sent."

"How many are there at present?" asked the Führer.

"More than ten thousand," said Himmler. "Most of them Poles."

"And here," continued Herr Bischoff, indicating a large area around the camp, "is what I call the zone of interest. About forty square kilometers of land that would be perfect for our needs."

"And all this is empty at the moment?" asked Hitler, running a finger along the map.

"No, mein Führer," replied Herr Bischoff, shaking his head. "It is occupied by landowners and farmers. I imagine we would have to consider buying the land from them."

"It can be confiscated," said the Obersturmbann-führer with an indifferent shrug. "The land will be requisitioned for the use of the Reich. The residents will simply have to understand."

"But—"

"Please continue, Herr Bischoff," said the Führer. "Ralf is correct. The land will be confiscated."

"Of course," he replied, and Pieter could see that the man was starting to perspire noticeably around his bald head. "Then here are the plans that I have designed for the second camp."

"And how large will it be?"

"Around four hundred and twenty-five acres."

"That big?" said the Führer, looking up, clearly impressed.

"I have been there myself, mein Führer," said Himmler, a proud expression on his face. "When I looked across at it, I knew that it would serve our needs."

"My good and loyal Heinrich," said Hitler with a smile, resting his hand on the other man's shoulder for a moment as he looked down at the plans. Himmler beamed with pleasure at the compliment.

"I've designed it to hold three hundred buildings," continued Herr Bischoff. "It will be the largest camp of its type anywhere in Europe. As you can see, I have used quite a formal pattern, but it will make it easier for the guards—"

"Of course, of course," said the Führer. "But how many prisoners will three hundred buildings hold? That does not sound like very much to me."

"But, mein Führer," said Herr Bischoff, opening his arms wide, "they are not small. Each one can hold any-where between six and seven hundred people."

Hitler looked up and closed one eye as he tried to calculate. "That would mean . . ."

"Two hundred thousand," said Pieter from behind the desk. Once again he had spoken without meaning to, but this time the Führer did not look at him angrily but with pleasure.

Turning back to the officers, he shook his head in amazement.

"Can that be right?" he asked.

"Yes, mein Führer," said Himmler. "Approximately."

"Extraordinary. Ralf, do you think you can oversee two hundred thousand prisoners?"

The Obersturmbannführer nodded without hesitation. "I will take great pride in doing so," he said.

"This is very good, gentlemen," said the Führer, nodding approvingly. "Now, how about security?"

"I propose dividing the camp into nine sections," said Herr Bischoff. "You can see here on my plans the separate areas. Over here, for example, the women's barracks. Over here, the men's. Each one will be surrounded by a wire fence—"

"An *electrified* wire fence," added Himmler.

"Yes, mein Reichsführer, of course. An electrified wire fence. It will be impossible for anyone to escape their particular section. But should the impossible happen, the entire camp will be surrounded by a second electrified wire fence. To try to escape will be suicide. And of course, there will be guard towers everywhere. Soldiers can be placed there, ready to shoot anyone who tries to run."

"And here?" asked the Führer, pointing to a place at the top of the map. "What is this? It says *Sauna*."

"I propose to create the steam chambers here," said Herr Bischoff. "To disinfect the clothes of the prisoners. By the time they arrive they will be covered in lice and other pests. We do not want disease to spread around the camp. We have our brave German soldiers to think of."

"I see," said Hitler, his eyes wandering over the complex design as if he was in search of something in particular.

"Each will be designed to look like a shower room," said Himmler. "Only there will not be water coming from the ceiling."

Pieter looked up from his notepad and frowned. "Excuse me, mein Reichsführer," he said.

"What is it, Pieter?" asked Hitler, turning around with a sigh.

"Forgive me, I think I must have misheard," said Pieter. "I thought you said that there would be no water coming from the showers."

All four men stared at the boy, and for a few moments no one spoke.

"No more interruptions, please, Pieter," said the Führer quietly, turning away.

"My apologies, mein Führer. Only I don't want to make an error in my transcript for Obersturmbannführer Höss."

"You have made no error. Now, Ralf, you were saying . . . the capacity?"

"To start with, about fifteen hundred per day. Within twelve months we can double that number."

"Very good. The important thing is that we are consistent in our turnover of prisoners. By the time we have won the war, we need to be sure that the world we inherit is pure for our purposes. You have created a thing of beauty, Karl."

The architect looked relieved and bowed his head. "Thank you, mein Führer."

"All that is left is to ask, when do we begin construction?"

"With your order, mein Führer, we can start work this week," said Himmler. "And if Ralf is as good as we all know he is, then the camp will be operational by October."

"You need have no worries about that, Heinrich," said the Obersturmbannführer with a bitter smile. "If the camp isn't ready by then, you may lock me up there, too, as my punishment."

Pieter felt his hand start to grow weary with all his writing, but something in the Obersturmbannführer's tone triggered a memory in his head and he looked up, staring at the camp commandant. He remembered now where he had seen him before. It was six years earlier, when he was hurrying toward the arrivals and

departures board in Mannheim, looking for the platform for the Munich train. The man in the earth-gray
uniform who had collided with him and pressed a boot
onto his fingers while he lay on the ground. The man
who would have broken his hand had his wife and children not appeared to take him away.

"This is very good," replied the Führer, smiling and
rubbing his hands together. "A great enterprise, gentlemen; perhaps the greatest the German people have ever
undertaken. Heinrich, the order is given. You may start
work on the camp immediately. Ralf, you will return
there immediately and oversee the operation."

"Of course, mein Führer."

Ralf saluted and walked over to Pieter, standing
before him and looking down.

"What?" asked Pieter.

"Your notes," replied the Obersturmbannführer.

Pieter handed him the notepad, on which he had
tried to scribble almost everything the four men ha
said, and the Obersturmbannführer glanced at it f a
moment before turning away, saying good-bye to a and
leaving the room.

"You can leave, too, Pieter," said the Führ Go outside and play if you like." n Führer,"

"I will go to my room and study d been spo-
replied Pieter, seething inside at the confidant who
ken to. One moment he was a tr

could sit in the most important seat in the land and take notes on the Führer's special project; the next he was being treated like a child. Well, he might be young, he decided, but at least he knew there was no point in building a shower room without water.

Chapter

12

Eva's Party

Katarina had started working in her father's stationery shop in Berchtesgaden just after her fifteenth birthday. It was 1944, and as Pieter made his way down the mountain to see her, he had, for once, decided not to wear the Hitlerjugend uniform of which he was so proud, but a pair of knee-length lederhosen, brown shoes, a white shirt, and dark tie. He knew that Katarina, for some inexplicable reason, didn't like uniforms, and he wanted to give her no cause to disapprove of him.

He hovered outside for almost an hour, trying to summon up the courage to go in. Of course, he saw her every day at school, but this was different; today he had a specific question to ask—though the idea of broaching it filled him with anxiety. He had thought about asking in a corridor between classes, but there was always a chance that one of their classmates would interrupt, so he had decided that this would be the best way.

Entering the shop, he saw her filling a rack with leather-bound notebooks, and when she turned around, he experienced the familiar blend of desire and distress that made him feel sick in the pit of his stomach. He desperately wanted her to like him but feared that he would never succeed; for the moment she saw who was standing there, her smile faded and she returned silently to her work.

"Good afternoon, Katarina," he said.

"Hello, Pieter," she replied, without turning around.

"It's such a beautiful day," he said. "Isn't Berchtesgaden beautiful at this time of year? Of course, you're beautiful throughout the year." He froze and shook his head, feeling the blush rise from his neck to his cheeks. "I mean, the town is beautiful throughout the year. It's a beautiful place. Whenever I am here in Berchtesgaden, I am always struck by its . . . by its . . ."

"By its beauty?" suggested Katarina, placing the last notebook on the rack and turning to him with a certain aloofness.

"Yes," he said, feeling downcast. He had prepared so hard for this conversation, and already it was going terribly wrong.

"Was there something you wanted, Pieter?" she asked.

"Yes, I need to buy some fountain pen nibs and ink, please."

"What kind?" asked Katarina, moving behind the counter and unlocking one of the glass cabinets.

"The best you have. They are to be used by the Führer himself, Adolf Hitler!"

"Of course," she said, with as little enthusiasm as she could muster. "You live with the Führer at the Berghof. You should mention it more often so people don't forget."

Pieter frowned. He was surprised to hear her say this as he thought he mentioned it often enough as it was. In fact, he sometimes thought that he shouldn't talk about it quite as much.

"Anyway, it's not a question of quality," she continued. "It's a question of nib type. Fine, medium, or broad. Or, if one's taste is a little more refined, one might try soft fine. Or Falcon. Or Sutab. Or Cors. Or—"

"Medium," said Pieter, who didn't like to be made to feel stupid but assumed that this was the safest option.

She opened a wooden box and looked up at him. "How many?"

"Half a dozen."

She nodded and began to count them out as Pieter leaned on the counter, attempting to appear casual.

"Would you mind not putting your hands on the glass?" she asked. "I only polished it a few minutes ago."

"Of course, my apologies," he said, standing up straight. "Although my hands are always clean. I am, after all, a highly valued member of the Hitlerjugend. And we pride ourselves on our good hygiene."

"Wait," said Katarina, stopping what she was doing and looking up at him as if he had just made a great revelation. "You're a member of the Hitlerjugend? Really?"

"Well, yes," he replied, baffled. "I wear my uniform to school every day."

"Oh, Pieter," she said, shaking her head and sighing.

"But you know that I'm a member of the Hitlerjugend!" he said in frustration.

"Pieter," she said, opening her arms wide over the array of pens and ink bottles in the glass cabinet before her, "you mentioned ink?"

"Ink?"

"Yes, you said you wanted to buy some."

"Oh, of course," said Pieter. "Six bottles, please."

"What color?"

"Four black, two red."

He looked around as a bell over the door rang, and a man entered carrying three large boxes of stock, for which Katarina signed, speaking to him in a much friendlier manner than she had addressed her classmate.

"More pens?" he asked when they were alone again, struggling to make conversation. This business of talking

216

to girls was a lot more complicated than he had anticipated.

"And paper. And other things."

"Isn't there anyone else who can help you?" he asked as she carried the boxes over to a corner and stacked them neatly.

"There used to be," she replied calmly, looking him directly in the eye. "A very nice lady named Ruth once worked here. For almost twenty years, in fact. She was like a second mother to me. But she's not here anymore."

"Oh no?" asked Pieter, feeling as if he was being led into a trap. "Why, what happened to her?"

"Who knows?" said Katarina. "She was taken away. As was her husband. And her three children. And her son's wife. And their two children. We've never heard from any of them since. She preferred a fountain pen with a soft fine nib. But then, she was a person of taste and sophistication. Unlike some people."

Pieter looked out the window, his annoyance at being so disrespected mingling with the aching desire that he felt for her. There was a boy who sat in the seat in front of him at school, Franz, who had recently begun a friendship with Gretchen Baffril; the whole school was abuzz with the gossip that they had kissed during a lunch break the previous week. And another boy, Martin Rensing, had invited Lenya Halle to his older sister's wedding a few weeks earlier, and a photograph had been circulated of them dancing together and holding hands later in the evening. How had they managed this when Katarina made things so difficult for him? And even now, as he looked out the window, Pieter saw a boy and a girl whom he did not recognize but who were around the same age as he and Katarina walking along, laughing about something. The boy fell into a squat and pretended to be an ape to entertain her, and she burst out laughing. They seemed at ease in each other's company. He couldn't imagine what that would be like.

"Jews, I suppose," he said, turning back to Katarina and spitting out the word in frustration. "This Ruth creature and her family. Jews, yes?"

"Yes," said Katarina, and as she leaned forward, he noticed how the top button of her blouse had almost come undone; he imagined that he could stare at it forever, the world silent and still around him, as he waited for the slight and welcoming breeze that might separate the fabric even more.

"Have you ever wanted to see the Berghof?" he asked after a moment, trying to ignore her rudeness as he looked back up.

She stared at him in surprise. "What?" she asked.

"I only ask because a party is to take place there this weekend. A birthday party for Fräulein Braun, who is the Führer's intimate friend. There will be many important people present. Perhaps you would like to take a break from your tedious life here and experience the excitement of such a grand occasion?"

Katarina raised an eyebrow and laughed a little. "I don't think so," she said.

"Of course, your father can come, too, if that's the problem," he added. "For propriety's sake."

"No," she said, shaking her head. "I simply don't want to, that's all. But thank you for the invitation."

"Your father can come where?" asked Herr Holzmann, emerging from a room at the back and wiping his hands on a towel, spreading a streak of black ink the shape of Italy. He stopped when he recognized Pieter; there were few people in Berchtesgaden who did not know who he was. "Good afternoon," he said, standing tall and pushing his chest out.

"Heil Hitler!" roared Pieter, clicking his heels together and performing his regular salute.

Katarina jumped in surprise and put a hand to her heart. Herr Holzmann attempted a similar salute, but it was far less professional than the boy's.

"Here are your nibs and your ink," said Katarina, handing him the package as he counted out his money. "Good-bye."

"Your father can come where?" repeated Herr Holzmann, standing next to his daughter now.

"Oberscharführer Fischer," said Katarina with a

sigh, "has invited me—or rather us—to a party at the Berghof this weekend. A birthday party."

"The Führer's birthday party?" her father asked, his eyes opening wide in surprise.

"No," said Pieter. "His friend. Fräulein Braun."

"But we'd be honored!" cried Herr Holzmann.

"Of course *you* would," replied Katarina. "You don't have a mind of your own anymore, do you?"

"Katarina!" he said, frowning at her before turning back to Pieter. "You'll have to forgive my daughter, Oberscharführer. She speaks before she thinks."

"At least I *do* think," she said. "Unlike you. When did you last have an opinion of your own that wasn't thrust at you by the—"

"*Katarina!*" he roared now, his face growing red. "You will speak with respect or you will go to your room. I'm sorry, Oberscharführer, my daughter is at a difficult age."

"He's the same age as I am," she muttered, and Pieter was surprised to notice that she was trembling.

"We'd be delighted to come," said Herr Holzmann, bowing his head a little in gratitude.

"Father, we can't. We have the shop to think about. Our customers. And you know how I feel about—"

"Don't worry about the shop," said her father, raising his voice. "Or the customers. Or anything else. Katarina, this is a great honor that the Oberscharführer has bestowed upon us." He looked back at Pieter. "What time should we arrive?"

"Any time after four," said Pieter, a little disappointed that he was coming at all. He would have preferred it if Katarina had come alone.

"We'll be there. And here, please—take your money back. You may present your items to the Führer as my gift."

"Thank you," said Pieter, smiling. "I'll see you both then. I'm looking forward to it. Good-bye, Katarina."

Stepping outside, he breathed a sigh of relief that the encounter was over and pocketed the money that Herr Holzmann had returned to him; after all, no one need ever know that he had been given the stationery supplies for free.

On the day of the party the Berghof was filled with some of the most important members of the Reich, most of whom seemed more intent on keeping out of the Führer's way than celebrating with Eva. Hitler had spent much of the morning locked in his office with Reichsführer Himmler and the minister for propaganda, Joseph Goebbels, and from the loud shouting coming through the door, Pieter could tell that he was not happy. He knew from the newspapers that the war was not going well. Italy had switched sides. The *Scharnhorst*, one of the most important vessels in the Kriegsmarine, had been sunk off the North Cape. And over the last few weeks the British had been bombing Berlin constantly. Now, as the party got started, the officers seemed relieved to be outside socializing, instead of having to defend themselves to an angry Führer.

Himmler was peering at the other guests through small round glasses, taking little nibbles from his food like a rat. He watched everyone, particularly those who were talking to the Führer, as if convinced that each conversation was about him. Goebbels sat on a deck chair on the veranda wearing a pair of dark glasses and turning his head to the sun. To Pieter, he looked like a skeleton with skin attached. Herr Speer, who had come to the Berghof several times in the past with designs for a remodeled postwar Berlin, looked as if he would rather be anywhere in the world than here. The atmosphere was strained, and whenever Pieter glanced toward Hitler, he saw a trembling man on the verge of losing his temper.

Throughout all this, he kept a close eye on the road that cut through the mountain, hoping that Katarina would show up as promised, but as four o'clock came and went, there was still no sign of her. He had put on a fresh uniform and was wearing aftershave that he'd stolen from Kempka's room, hoping this would be enough to impress her.

Eva was moving from group to group anxiously, accepting congratulations and gifts and, as usual, mostly ignoring Pieter, who had presented her with a copy of *The Magic Mountain*, bought with his meager savings. "How thoughtful," she had said, placing it on a side table before moving on, and he imagined that Herta would probably pick it up at some point later and put it on one of the shelves in the library, unread.

Between staring down the mountain and observing the party, the thing that interested Pieter most was a woman walking around with a cine-camera in her hands, pointing it in the direction of the guests and asking them to say a few words. However chatty they had all been with one another before, when she appeared, they grew self-conscious and seemed unwilling to be filmed, turning away or covering their faces with their hands. Occasionally she would take shots of the house or the mountain, and Pieter found himself intrigued by her. At one point she stepped into the center of a conversation between Goebbels and Himmler, and they stopped talking immediately, turning to stare at her without a word; she walked off in the opposite direction. Spotting the boy standing on his own, looking down the mountainside, she came over to join him.

"Not thinking of jumping, are you?" she asked.

"No, of course not," said Pieter. "Why would I even contemplate such a thing?"

"I was joking," she replied. "You look very smart in your costume."

"It's not a costume," he said irritably. "It's a uniform."

"I'm just teasing," she said. "What's your name, anyway?"

"Pieter," he said. "And you?"

"Leni."

"What are you doing with that?" he asked, pointing at the camera.

"Making a film."

"For who?"

"For whoever wants to watch it."

"I presume you're married to one of them?" he asked, nodding in the direction of the officers.

"Oh no," she said. "None of them are interested in anyone but themselves."

Pieter frowned. "So where's your husband?" he asked.

"I don't have one. Why, are you proposing?"

"Of course not."

"You're a little young for me anyway—what are you, fourteen?"

"Fifteen," he said angrily. "And I wasn't proposing, I was simply asking a question, that's all."

"As it happens, I'm getting married later this month."

Pieter said nothing and turned away, looking down.

"What's so interesting down there?" asked Leni, looking over now, too. "Are you waiting for someone?"

"No," he said. "Who would I be waiting for? Everyone who matters is already here."

"So will you let me film you?"

He shook his head. "I'm a soldier," he said. "Not an actor."

"Well, you're neither at the moment," she said. "You're just a boy wearing a uniform. But you're handsome, that's for sure. You'll look good on film."

Pieter stared at her. He wasn't accustomed to being spoken to like this and didn't care for it. Didn't she understand how important he was? He opened his mouth to speak, but as he did so, he noticed a car turning the corner at the top of the road and heading in his direction. He watched it and started to smile when he saw who was sitting in it, before composing his features again.

"Now I see what you were waiting for," said Leni, holding the camera up and filming the car as it drove along. "Or rather, *who* you were waiting for."

He felt an urge to rip the camera from her hands and throw it down the Obersalzberg, but simply smoothed down his jacket to ensure that he was neatly attired, and made his way over to greet his guests.

"Herr Holzmann," he said, performing a polite bow as the two townspeople emerged. "Katarina. I'm so glad that you could make it. Welcome to the Berghof."

*   *   *

Later that day, when Pieter realized that he hadn't seen Katarina for some time, he went inside the house, where he discovered her staring at some paintings that hung on the walls. The afternoon had not gone particularly well so far. Herr Holzmann had done his best to converse with the Nazi officers, but he was unsophisticated, and Pieter knew that they were laughing at his attempts to ingratiate himself with them. He seemed frightened, however, by the presence of the Führer and stayed as far away from him as he could. Pieter despised him, wondering how a grown man could come to a party and behave like a boy.

His conversation with Katarina had been even more difficult. She refused even to pretend that she was happy to be there, and it was obvious that she wanted to leave as soon as possible. Upon being introduced to the Führer, she had behaved respectfully but with none of the awe that Pieter had expected.

"So you're our young Pieter's girlfriend?" asked Hitler, smiling a little as he looked her up and down.

"Certainly not," she replied. "We're in the same class in school, that's all."

"But look at how enamored he is," said Eva, coming over, ready to join in the teasing. "We didn't think Pieter was even interested in girls yet."

"Katarina is just a friend," said Pieter, blushing furiously.

"I'm not even that," she said, smiling sweetly.

"Ah, you say that now," said the Führer, "but I can see a spark there. It will not be long before it is ignited. The future Frau Fischer perhaps?"

Katarina said nothing but looked as if she was ready to explode in anger. When the Führer and Eva moved on, Pieter tried to engage her in conversation about some of the other young people they knew from Berchtesgaden, but she gave almost nothing away, as if she didn't want him to know too much about her opinions. When he asked her what her favorite battle of the war was so far, she stared at him as if he was crazy.

"The one where the least number of people died," she said.

The afternoon had progressed like that, with his trying his best to engage her and being rebuffed at every turn. But, he told himself, perhaps that was because there were so many people outside. Now that they were alone together inside the house, he hoped that she might be a little more forthcoming.

"Have you enjoyed the party?" he asked.

"I'm not sure anyone here is enjoying themselves," she said.

He glanced up at the painting that she had been looking at. "I didn't know you were interested in art," he said.

"Well," she said, "I am."

"Then this piece must please you very much."

Katarina shook her head. "It's ghastly," she replied, looking around at the paintings. "They all are. I would have thought that a man with the Führer's power would have chosen something a little better from the museums."

Pieter's eyes opened wide, horrified by what she had said. He raised a finger and pointed at the artist's signature in the lower right-hand corner of the frame.

"Oh," she said, momentarily chastened, perhaps a little nervous. "Well, it doesn't matter who painted them. They're still terrible."

He took her roughly by the arm and pulled her along the corridor and into his bedroom, slamming the door behind him.

"What are you doing?" she asked, pulling free.

"Protecting you," he said. "You can't say things like that here, don't you understand? You will get into trouble."

"I didn't know *he* painted them," she said, throwing her hands up in the air.

"Well, now you do. So keep your mouth shut in the future, Katarina, until you understand what you're talking about. And stop talking down to me. I invited you here, to a place a girl like you would never usually get to visit. It's time you showed me a little respect."

She stared at him, and he could see a growing fear

behind her eyes that she was doing her best to control. He wasn't sure if he welcomed that or not. "Don't speak to me like that," she said quietly.

"I'm sorry," replied Pieter, stepping closer to her now. "It's only because I care about you, that's all. I don't want to see any harm come to you."

"You don't even know me."

"I've known you for years now!"

"You don't know me at all."

He sighed. "Perhaps not," he said. "But I'd like to change that. If you'd let me."

He reached forward and ran a finger along her cheek as she took a step back toward the wall.

"You're so very beautiful," he whispered, surprised to hear such words emerging from his mouth.

"Stop, Pieter," she said, turning away.

"But why?" he asked, leaning in closer so the scent of her perfume almost overwhelmed him. "It's what I want." He used one hand to turn her face back to him and leaned in to kiss her.

"Get off me," she said, using both hands to push him away, and he stumbled backward, an expression of surprise on his face as he tripped over a chair and ended up on the floor.

"What?" he asked, startled and confused.

"Keep your hands off me, do you hear?" She opened the door but didn't yet leave, turning around to look at him as he picked himself up. "There's nothing in the world that would make me want to kiss you."

He shook his head in disbelief. "But don't you understand what an honor it would be for you?" he asked. "Don't you know how important I am?"

"Of course I do," she replied. "You're the little boy in the lederhosen who comes to buy ink for the Führer's fountain pens. How could I possibly underestimate your value?"

"There's more to me than that," he snarled, standing up and walking over to her. "You just have to let me show you some kindness, that's all." He reached out for her again, and this time she slapped him hard across the face, a ring on her finger catching against his skin and producing a spot of blood. He yelped and put a hand to his cheek, looking at her with fury in his eyes, and advanced again, this time pushing her against the wall and holding her there.

"Who do you think you are?" he asked, his face pressed close to hers. "You think you can reject me? Most girls in Germany would kill to be in your position right now."

He moved in to kiss her again, and this time, with his body pressed so close to hers, she was unable to pull away. She struggled and tried to push him off, but he was too strong for her. His left hand ran down her body, groping her through her dress, and although she tried to cry out for help, his right hand was pressed against her mouth, silencing her. He felt her growing weak beneath the pressure and knew that she would be unable to fight him off for much longer; he could do anything he wanted to her. A small voice in his head told him to stop. Another, a louder one, told him to take what he wanted.

A force from nowhere knocked Pieter back onto the floor, and before he knew what was happening, he found himself lying prostrate while someone sat on top of him, pressing the sharp edge of a carving knife against his throat. He tried to swallow but could feel the blade touching his skin and didn't want to risk being cut.

"You lay another finger on that poor girl," whispered Emma, "and I will slit your throat from ear to ear. I don't care what happens to me afterward. Do you understand me, Pieter?" He said nothing, letting his eyes dart back and forth between the woman and the girl. "Tell me you understand me, Pieter—say it now, or so help me—"

"Yes, I understand you," he hissed, and she stood up, leaving him lying there, rubbing his throat and inspecting his fingers for blood. He glanced up, humiliated, his eyes filled with hatred. "You've made a big mistake, Emma," he said quietly.

"I don't doubt it," she said. "But it's nothing like the mistake your poor aunt made the day she decided to take you in." Her face softened for a moment, and she stared down at him. "What happened to you, Pierrot?"

she asked. "You were such a sweet boy when you first came here. Is it really that easy for the innocent to be corrupted?"

Pieter said nothing. He wanted to curse her, to bring his fury down upon her, upon both of them, but something in the way she stared at him, the mixture of pity and contempt on her face, brought some memory of the boy he had once been back to his mind. Katarina was weeping now, and he looked away, willing them both to leave him alone. He didn't want their eyes on him anymore.

Only when he heard their footsteps making their way down the corridor and heard Katarina telling her father that it was time to go did he struggle to his feet once again. But this time, instead of returning to the party, he closed the door and lay down on his bed, trembling slightly; and then, without quite knowing why, he began to cry.

Chapter

13

The Darkness and the Light

The house was empty and silent.

Outside, the trees that covered the mountains of the Obersalzberg were bursting into life, and as Pieter walked the grounds, carelessly tossing a ball that had once belonged to Blondi, he found it hard to imagine that there could be such serenity up here while the world below, which had spent almost six years being brutalized and torn asunder, was in the final throes of another destructive war.

He had turned sixteen a couple of months earlier and been allowed to exchange the uniform of the Hitlerjugend for the field-gray fatigues of a junior soldier, although whenever he asked to be assigned to a battalion, the Führer had brushed him aside and told him that he was too busy for such inconsequential appointments. More than half his life had been spent in the Berghof, and when he tried to think about the people he had known in Paris during his childhood, it was a struggle even to remember their names or faces.

He had heard rumors about the things that were happening to Jews around Europe and knew at last why his aunt Beatrix had insisted that he should not talk about his friend when he came to live there. He wondered whether Anshel was alive or dead, whether his mother had managed to sneak them both away to a safer place, and whether D'Artagnan had gone with them.

The thought of his dog made him fling the ball over the side of the mountain, and he watched as it soared through the air before disappearing into the heart of a clump of trees some distance away.

Looking down at the road, he remembered the night he had first come here, frightened and lonely, while Beatrix and Ernst drove him to his new home, trying to convince him that he would be safe and happy there. He closed his eyes at the memory and shook his head, as if the recollection of what had happened to them and how he had betrayed them was something that could be forgotten. But he was starting to realize that it wasn't that simple.

There were others, too. Emma, the cook who had shown him nothing but kindness through his early years at the Berghof, but whose insult at Eva Braun's party could not have gone unpunished by him. He had spoken to the Führer of what she had done, understated his role in the events of that afternoon, and exaggerated the things she had said to make her sound like a traitor, and a day later she had been taken away by the soldiers without even enough time to pack a bag. Where they had taken her, he didn't know. She had wept as she was led toward the car, and he had last seen her sitting in the backseat with her head in her hands as she was driven away. Ange had gone soon afterward, of her own volition. Only Herta had stayed.

The Holzmanns, too, had been forced to leave Berchtesgaden, the stationery shop that Katarina's father had run for so many years closed down and sold. He hadn't known anything about this until a visit to the town led him to the store, where the windows were boarded up and a sign on the front door stated that it was soon to become a grocery store. When he asked the owner of the shop next door what had happened to them, she had looked at him without any fear in her eyes and shook her head.

"You're the boy who lives up there, aren't you?" she asked, cocking her head in the direction of the mountains.

"That's right, yes," he replied.

"Then *you're* what happened to them," she said.

He had been too ashamed to say anything and left without another word. The truth was that he was filled with regrets but had no one in whom he could confide. Despite the injury he had done her, he had hoped that Katarina would listen to him and let him apologize—and, if she could, allow him to talk about the life he had lived so far, the things he had done and seen, that perhaps he might then find some form of forgiveness.

But the possibility of that was gone now.

Two months earlier, when the Führer had stayed at the Berghof for the final time, he had seemed like a mere shadow of the man he had once been. Gone was the supreme confidence, the power to command, the absolute belief in his own destiny and the destiny of his country. Instead, he had been paranoid and angry, trembling and muttering to himself as he wandered the hallways, the slightest noise enough to provoke his rage. On one occasion he had all but destroyed everything in his office; on another he had struck Pieter with the back of his hand when the boy came to see whether he could bring him anything. He stayed up late into the night, mumbling under his breath, cursing his generals, cursing the British and the Americans, cursing everyone he felt was responsible for his downfall. Everyone, that is, except himself.

There had been no good-byes between the two. A group of Schutzstaffel officers had simply arrived one morning and locked themselves in the study with the Führer for a long discussion, and then he had marched out, ranting and raging, before throwing himself into the backseat of his car, screaming at Kempka to take him away, to take him anywhere, to get him off this mountaintop once and for all. Eva had been forced to run after him as the car pulled out of the driveway, and the last Pieter saw of her was her running down the mountain in its wake, waving her arms and shouting, her blue dress blowing in the wind as she disappeared beyond the curve of the hills.

The soldiers disappeared soon after, which left only Herta, and then one morning Pieter discovered her packing her bags, too.

"Where will you go?" he asked, standing in the doorway of her room, and she turned to look at him, shrugging her shoulders.

"Back to Vienna, I expect," she said. "My mother is still there. At least, I think she is. I don't know whether the trains are running, of course, but I'll find my way."

"What will you tell her?"

"Nothing. I will never speak of this place again, Pieter. You would be wise to do the same. Leave now, before the armies arrive. You're still young. No one needs to know the terrible things you've done. That we've all done."

He felt the words like a shot to his heart and could scarcely believe the look of absolute conviction on her face as she condemned them both. Taking her by the arm as she passed him, he spoke in a whisper, remembering the first night he had met her nine years before, when he had been mortified that she would see him naked in the bathtub.

"Will there be any forgiveness, Herta?" he asked. "The newspapers . . . the things they're saying already . . . will there be any forgiveness for me?"

She carefully released his hand from her elbow. "Do you think that I didn't know the plans that were being made up here on this mountaintop?" she said. "The things that were being discussed in the Führer's office? There will be no forgiveness for any of us."

"But I was just a child," pleaded Pieter. "I didn't know anything. I didn't understand."

She shook her head and took his face in her hands. "Look at me, Pieter," she said. "Look at me." He looked up, tears in his eyes. "Don't ever pretend that you didn't know what was going on here. You have eyes and you have ears. And you sat in that room on many occasions, taking notes. You heard it all. You saw it all. You knew it all. And you also know the things you are responsible for." She hesitated, but it needed to be said. "The deaths you have on your conscience. But you're a young man still; you're only sixteen. You have many years ahead of you to come to terms with your complicity in these matters. Just don't ever tell yourself that you didn't know." She released him now from her grip. "That would be the worst crime of all."

She picked up her suitcase and made her way to the

doorway. He watched her, framed by the sunlight that was bursting through the trees.

"How will you get down?" he asked, calling after her, wishing she wouldn't leave him there alone. "There's no one else left. No car to take you."

"I'll walk," she said, turning away and disappearing out of sight.

The newspapers continued to be delivered, the local suppliers afraid to stop calling in case the Führer returned and took out his displeasure on them. There were some who believed that the war might still be won. And then there were those who were ready to face reality. In the town, Pieter heard rumors that the Führer and Eva had moved into a secret bunker in Berlin, along with the most important members of the National Socialist Party, and were plotting their return, masterminding the manner in which they would emerge even stronger than before, with a certain plan for victory. And again, there were some who believed that and some who didn't. But still the newspapers kept coming.

Seeing the last soldiers preparing to leave Berchtesgaden, Pieter approached them, asking what he should do and where he should go.

"You're wearing a uniform, aren't you?" said one, looking him up and down. "Why don't you use it for once?"

"Pieter doesn't fight," said his fellow officer. "He just likes to dress up."

And with that, they started to laugh at him, and watching as they drove off, he felt that his humiliation was complete.

Now the little boy who had been brought to the mountain in shorts began to ascend it for the last time.

He stayed there, uncertain what to do next. Reading the papers, he followed the arrival of the Allies into the heart of Germany and wondered when the enemy would come for him. A few days before the end of the month, a plane flew overhead, a British Lancaster bomber, and dropped two bombs onto the side of the Obersalzberg, just missing the Berghof itself but sending enough debris back to shatter most of the windows. Pieter had been hiding inside the house, in the Führer's own study, and as the glass exploded all around him, hundreds of tiny shards flew toward his face, sending him hurtling to the floor, screaming in terror. Only when the sound of the planes had gone did he feel safe enough to stand up and make his way into the bathroom, where he was greeted by his bloodied countenance in the mirror. He spent the rest of the afternoon trying to remove as much glass as possible; he feared that the scars would never go away.

The last newspaper arrived on May 2, and the headline on the front page told him everything he needed to know. The Führer was dead. Goebbels was gone, too, that awful skeletal man, along with his wife and children. Eva had bitten into a cyanide capsule; Hitler had put a gun to his head. The worst of it was that before the cyanide was taken, the Führer decided that it needed to be tested, to ensure that it really worked. The last thing he wanted was for Eva to be left writhing in agony and captured by the enemy. He wanted her to have a swift release.

And so he tried a capsule out on Blondi. And it worked, quickly and efficiently.

Pieter felt almost nothing as he read the newspaper. He stood outside the Berghof and looked across at the landscape that surrounded him. He glanced down toward Berchtesgaden and then toward Munich, remembering the train journey where he had first encountered members of the Hitlerjugend. And finally his eyes turned in the direction of Paris, the city of his birth, a place that he had all but disowned in his desire to be important. But he wasn't French anymore, he realized. Nor was he German. He was nothing. He had no home, no family, and he deserved none.

He wondered whether he could live there forever. Hide away on the mountainside like a hermit and live off whatever he found in the forests. Perhaps he would never need to see humans again. Let them all get on with their lives down there, he thought. Let them continue with their fighting and their warring and their shooting and their killing, and perhaps they would leave him out of it. He would never have to speak again. He would never have to explain himself. No one would ever look into his eyes and see the things he had done or recognize the person he had become.

For an afternoon, the idea seemed like a good one.

And then the soldiers came.

It was late in the afternoon of May 4, and Pieter was picking up stones from the gravel driveway, trying to dislodge a tin can from its perch. The silence of the Obersalzberg began slowly to be infiltrated by a deep sound that rose from the base of the mountain to where he stood. As it grew louder, he stared over the side to where a troop of soldiers were ascending, not wearing German uniforms, but American ones. They were coming for him.

He thought of escaping into the forest, but there was no point in running and nowhere to run to anyway. He was left with no choice. He would wait for them.

He went back inside the house and sat in the living room, but as they came closer, he began to feel afraid and went out into the hallway in search of a hiding place. In the corner was a small closet, barely big enough to accommodate him, but he climbed inside and closed the door behind him. A little string hung from just above his head, and when he pulled it, a light came on, illuminating the space. There were only some old wash-cloths and dustpans in there, but something was poking into his back and he reached around to see what it was. Pulling it out, he was surprised to find that a book had been carelessly thrown in, and he turned it to look at the title. *Emil and the Detectives.* He pulled the light cord again, condemning himself to darkness.

Voices filled the house now, and he could hear the boots of the soldiers as they made their way into the room. They were calling out to one another in a language he didn't understand, laughing and whooping with delight as they looked inside his bedroom, the Führer's room, the maids' rooms. Inside what had once been his aunt Beatrix's room. He heard bottles being opened, corks being popped. And then he heard two sets of boots making their way down the corridor toward him.

"What's in here?" asked one of the soldiers in an American accent, and before Pieter could reach out to hold it closed, the door to the closet swung open, letting in a burst of light that forced him to shut his eyes quickly.

The soldiers let out a cry, and he heard their guns cocking as they pointed them at him. He cried out in return, and a moment later there were four, six, ten, a dozen, an entire company of men gathered around, pointing their guns at the boy hiding in the darkness.

"Don't hurt me," cried Pieter, curling himself into a ball, covering his head with his hands, wishing for all the world that he could make himself so small that he would simply disappear into nothingness. "Please don't hurt me."

And before he could speak again, an unknown number of hands reached into the darkness and pulled him back out into the light.

EPILOGUE

Chapter

14

A Boy Without a Home

Having spent so many years in near isolation at the top of the Obersalzberg, Pieter struggled to adjust to life in the Golden Mile Camp near Remagen, where he was taken immediately after his capture. He was told on his arrival that he was not a prisoner of war, since the war was now officially over, but part of a group known as the "disarmed enemy forces" instead.

"What's the difference?" asked a man standing near him in the line.

"Means we don't have to follow the Geneva Convention," replied one of the American guards, spitting on the ground as he took a packet of cigarettes from his jacket pocket. "So don't expect a free ride here, Fritz."

Incarcerated with a quarter of a million captured German soldiers, Pieter made a decision as he entered the gates that he would talk to no one and employ only the few bits of sign language he recalled from his childhood to pretend that he was deaf and mute, a charade that worked so well that soon no one even looked in his direction anymore, let alone spoke to him. It was as if he didn't exist. Which was exactly how he wanted it to be.

In his section of the camp, there were more than a thousand men, ranging from officers of the Wehrmacht, who still held nominal authority over their subordinates, to members of the Hitlerjugend, some even younger than Pieter himself, although the ones who looked particularly youthful were released within a few days. The hut where he slept contained two hundred men who crowded onto cots that held only a quarter of their number, and most nights he found himself trying to find an empty space by a wall where he could lie down with his jacket rolled under his head, hoping to get a few hours' sleep.

Some soldiers, mostly the senior ones, were interrogated to find out what they had done during the war, and having been discovered in the Berghof, Pieter was questioned about his activities many times but continued to feign deafness, writing on notepaper the true story of how he had come to leave Paris and find himself in the care of his aunt. The authorities sent in different officers to question him, hoping to find a discrepancy in his tale, but as he always told the truth there was nothing they could do to catch him out.

"And your aunt?" one of the soldiers asked him.

"What happened to her? She wasn't at the Berghof when you were discovered."

Pieter held his pen over the notepad and tried to steady his trembling hand. *She died*, he wrote finally, unable to look the man in the eye as he passed the pad across.

Fights broke out occasionally. Some of the men were embittered by their defeat; others were more stoical. One evening a man who Pieter knew—from the gray woolen Fliegermütze side-cap he wore—had been a member of the Luftwaffe began denouncing the National Socialist Party, sparing nothing in his contempt for the Führer. An officer from the Wehrmacht marched over and slapped him across the face with his glove, calling him a traitor and the reason they had lost the war. For ten minutes they rolled around on the floor, striking each other, kicking and punching, while the other men formed a circle around them, cheering them on, excited by the brutality, which came as a relief from the tedium of the Golden Mile. In the end, the soldier lost to the airman, a result that divided the hut, but so severe were both their injuries that by the next morning they had disappeared and Pieter never saw either of them again.

Finding himself standing by the kitchens one afternoon when none of the soldiers were standing guard, he crept in and stole a loaf of bread, smuggling it back to the hut inside his shirt and nibbling on it throughout the day, his stomach growling in delight at this unexpected offering; but he had only eaten half of it before an Oberleutnant a little older than he was noticed what he was doing and came over to take it from him. Pieter tried to fight him off, but the man was too strong for him, and eventually Pieter gave up, retreating to his corner like a caged animal aware of a stronger aggressor, trying to clear his head of all thoughts. Emptiness was the state he longed for. Emptiness and amnesia.

From time to time English-language newspapers would circulate among the huts, and those who could understand them would translate, telling the gathered men what had been taking place in their country since the surrender. Peter heard how the architect Albert Speer had been sentenced to prison; how Leni Riefenstahl, the lady who had filmed him on the terrace of the Berghof during Eva's party, claimed to have known nothing of what the Nazis were doing but was being held in various French and American detention camps nevertheless. The Obersturmbannführer who had once stood on Pierrot's hand in Mannheim station and had subsequently come to the Berghof with his arm in a sling to take control of one of the death camps had been captured by the Allied forces and went with them without complaint. Of Herr Bischoff, who had designed the camp in his so-called zone of interest, he heard nothing, but he learned how the gates had been opened at

Auschwitz, Bergen-Belsen, and Dachau, at Buchenwald and Ravensbrück, as far east as Jasenovac in Croatia, as far north as Bredtvet in Norway, and to the south in Sajmište, and how the inmates had been released to return to their shattered homes, having lost parents, brothers, sisters, uncles, aunts, and children. He listened intently as the details of what had gone on in these places were revealed to the world and grew more numb as he tried to understand the cruelty of which he had been a part. When he couldn't sleep, which was often, he lay staring at the ceiling, thinking: *I am responsible.*

And then one morning he was released. About five hundred men were brought to the courtyard to be told that they could return to their families. The men looked surprised, as if they suspected it might be a trap of some sort, making their way toward the gates nervously. Only when they were a mile or two away from the camp and certain that they were not being followed did they begin to relax, at which point they looked at one another, confused by their liberation after so many years of army life, and wondered, *What do we do now?*

Pieter spent much time in the following years moving from place to place, seeing the destructive signs of the war in the faces of the people and the landmarks of the cities. From Remagen, he traveled north toward Cologne, where he saw how badly the city had crumbled beneath the bombs of the Royal Air Force. Everywhere he turned, buildings were half destroyed and streets were impassable, although the great cathedral at the heart of the Domkloster remained standing despite the number of hits it had taken. From there, he made his way west toward Antwerp, where he found work for a time at the busy port that stretched along the waterfront, living in an attic room overlooking the Schelde River.

He made a friend—a rare thing for him as the other dockyard workers had him down as something of a loner—but this friend, a young man of his own age named Daniel, seemed to share something of Pieter's loneliness. Even in the heat, Daniel always wore a long-sleeved shirt when everyone else was bare-chested, and they teased him about it, saying that he was so shy he would never be able to find a girlfriend.

Occasionally they ate dinner together or went for a drink, and Daniel never mentioned his wartime experiences any more than Pieter himself did.

Once, late one evening in a bar, Daniel mentioned that it would have been his parents' thirtieth wedding anniversary that day.

"Would have been?" asked Pieter.

"They're both dead," replied Daniel quietly.

"I'm sorry."

"My sisters, too," confided Daniel, his finger rubbing

at an invisible mark on the table between them. "And my brother."

Pieter said nothing but knew immediately why Daniel always wore long sleeves and refused to remove his shirt. Beneath those sleeves, he knew, was a number scarred into the skin, and Daniel, scarcely able to live with the memory of what had happened to his family, was forced to see an eternal reminder every time he looked down.

The next day, Pieter wrote a letter to his employer, resigning from the shipyard, and went on his way without even saying good-bye.

He took a train north to Amsterdam, where he lived for the next six years, changing vocations entirely as he trained as a teacher, securing a position at a school near the train station. He never spoke of his past, making few friends outside his job and spending most of his time alone in his room.

One Sunday afternoon, taking a stroll through the Westerpark, he stopped to listen to a musician playing the violin beneath a tree and was transported back to his childhood in Paris—those carefree days when he had visited the Tuileries Garden with his father. A crowd had gathered, and when the performer stopped to run a cake of rosin across the strings of his bow, a young woman stepped forward to throw a few coins into his upturned hat. Turning back, she glanced in Pieter's direction, and as their eyes met, he felt his stomach contort in pain. Although they had not met in many years, he knew her instantly, and it was clear that she recognized him, too. The last time he saw her she had been running in tears from his bedroom in the Berghof, the fabric of her blouse ripped at the shoulder where he had pulled at it before Emma had sent him sprawling to the floor. She walked over now without any fear in her eyes and stood before him, even more beautiful than he remembered her from their shared youth. Her gaze didn't shift; she simply stared at him as if words were unnecessary, until he could bear it no longer and lowered his eyes to the ground in shame. He hoped that she would walk away, but she didn't. She stood her ground, and when he dared to look up again, she wore an expression on her face of such contempt that he wished he could simply disappear into thin air. Turning away without a word, he made his way home.

By the end of the week, he had resigned his position at the school and understood that the moment he had put off for so long had finally come.

It was time to go home.

The first place Pieter visited when he returned to France was the orphanage in Orléans, but when he arrived, it was no longer fully standing. During the occupation, it had been taken over by the Nazis, the children scattered to the winds as it became a center of operations for the Germans. When it became clear that the war was coming to an end, the Nazis had fled the building, destroying portions of it as they left, but the walls were strong and it didn't completely fall apart. It would have taken a lot of money to rebuild it, and as yet no one had stepped forward to re-create the haven it had once been for children who had no families of their own.

Walking into the office where he had first met the Durand sisters, Pieter looked for the glass cabinet that had held their brother's medal, but it was gone, along with the sisters themselves.

The war records department, however, led him to discover that Hugo, who had bullied him when he lived there, had died a hero. As a teenage boy, he had resisted the occupying forces and run several dangerous missions that saved the lives of many of his compatriots before being discovered in the act of planting a bomb near the same orphanage where he had grown up on the day a German general had come to visit. He was lined up against a wall and reportedly refused the blindfold as the soldiers pointed their weapons at him, wanting to look his executioners in the eye as he fell.

Of Josette he could find no trace. Another missing child of the war, he realized, whose fate he would never know.

Arriving back in Paris at last, he spent his first night writing a letter to a lady who lived in Leipzig. He described in detail the actions he had taken one Christmas Eve when he was a boy, and said that while he understood that he could not expect to be forgiven, he wanted her to know how eternally regretful he would be.

He received a simple, polite reply from Ernst's sister, who told him that she had been tremendously proud when her brother had become chauffeur to such a great man as Adolf Hitler and considered his actions in attempting to assassinate the Führer a stain on her family's proud history.

"You did what any patriot would have done," she wrote, and Pieter read the letter in astonishment, realizing that time might move on, but the ideas of some people never would.

One afternoon a few weeks later, he found himself strolling past a bookshop in the Montmartre district, and he stopped to look at a display in the window. It had been many years since he had read a novel—the last had been *Emil and the Detectives*—but there was something there that caught his eye and made him go inside to lift the book from its stand, turning it around to look at the photograph of the author on the back.

The novel was written by Anshel Bronstein, the boy who had lived in the flat below him when they were children. Of course, he remembered, he had wanted to be a writer. It seemed that his ambition had come true.

He bought the book and read it over the course of two evenings before making his way to the office of the publisher, where he said that he was an old friend of Anshel's and would like to contact him. He was given the writer's address and informed that he would probably find him at home as Monsieur Bronstein spent every afternoon there, writing.

The flat was not far away, but Pieter made his way there slowly, worried about the reception that he might receive. He didn't know whether Anshel would be able to listen to the story of his life, whether he would be able to stomach it, but he knew that he had to try. After all, it was he who had stopped responding to Anshel's letters, telling him that they were no longer friends and that he should stop writing to him. Knocking on the door, he didn't even know whether Anshel would remember him.

———————————

But of course, I knew him immediately.

Usually, I don't like it when someone comes to my door while I'm working. It's not easy to write a novel. It takes time and patience, and to be distracted even for a moment can lead to the loss of an entire day's work. And that afternoon, I was writing an important scene and was irritated by the interruption, but it did not take more than a moment for me to recognize the man standing at my door, trembling slightly as he looked at me. The years had passed—they had not been kind to either of us—but I would have known him anywhere.

Pierrot, I signed, using my fingers to make the symbol of the dog, kind and loyal, with which I had christened him as a boy.

Anshel, he signed in reply, making the symbol of the fox.

We stood staring at each other for what felt like a very long time, and then I stood back, opening the door to invite him inside. He sat down opposite me in my study and looked around at the photographs on the walls. The picture of my mother, from whom I had hidden when the soldiers rounded up the Jews on our street and whom I had last seen being bundled into a truck with so many of our neighbors. The picture of D'Artagnan, his dog, my dog, the dog that had tried to attack one of the Nazis as he captured her and been shot for his bravery. The picture of the family who had taken me in and hidden me, claiming me as their own despite the trouble it had caused them.

He said nothing for a long time, and I decided to wait until he was ready. And then finally he said that he had a story to tell: a story of a boy who had started out with love and decency in his heart but had found himself corrupted by power. The story of a boy who had committed crimes with which he would have to live forever, a boy who had hurt people who loved him and been a party to the deaths of those who only ever showed him kindness, who had sacrificed his right to his own name and would have to spend a lifetime trying to earn it back. The story of a man who wanted to find some way to make amends for his actions and who would always remember the words of a maid named Herta, who had told him never to pretend that he hadn't known what was going on, that such a lie would be the worst crime of all.

"Do you remember when we were children?" he asked me. "Like you, I had stories to tell but could never get the words down on the page. I would have an idea, but only you could find the words. You told me that even though you might have written it, it was still my story."

"I remember," I said.

"Could we be children again, do you think?"

I shook my head and smiled. "Too much has happened for that to be possible," I told him. "But you can tell me what happened after you left Paris, of course. And after that, we shall see."

"This story will take some time to tell," Pierrot told me, "and when you hear it, you might despise me. You might even want to kill me, but I am going to tell you, and you can do with it what you will. Perhaps you will write about it. Or perhaps you think it would be better forgotten."

I went over to my desk and set my novel aside. It was a trivial thing, after all, compared with this, and I could return to it one day, when I had heard everything he had to say. And then, taking a fresh notebook and fountain pen from my cabinet, I turned back to my old friend and used the only voice I have ever had—my hands—to sign three simple words that I knew he would understand.

Let us begin.

Acknowledgments

Every novel I write is improved immeasurably by the advice and support of wonderful friends and colleagues around the world. Many thanks to my agents, Simon Trewin, Eric Simonoff, Anne Marie Blumenhagen, and all at WME; and my editors, Annie Eaton and Natalie Doherty at Random House Children's Books in the UK; Laura Godwin at Henry Holt in the USA; Kristin Cochrane, Martha Leonard, and the wonderful team at Random House Canada; and all those who publish my novels around the world.

Thanks, too, to my husband and best friend, Con.

The final sections of this novel were written at my alma mater, the University of East Anglia, Norwich, during autumn 2014, where I was teaching on the Creative Writing MA. For reminding me how wonderful it is to be a writer and forcing me to think about fiction in different ways, big thanks to some great writers of the future: Anna Pook, Bikram Sharma, Emma Miller, Graham Rushe, Molly Morris, Rowan Whiteside, Tatiana Strauss, and Zakia Uddin.

GOFISH

JOHN BOYNE

What did you want to be when you grew up?
Happy. Which meant that I knew I had to spend my life with books. I only ever wanted to be a writer.

When did you realize you wanted to be a writer?
Around the age of seven or eight. I had a bit of a stationery fetish—I still do—and loved writing stories on elegant paper with fancy pens.

What's your most embarrassing childhood memory?
I was an altar boy and was so frightened by the consequences of showing up for the wrong Mass one day that I burst into tears on the altar and had to be carried off.

What's your favorite childhood memory?
Our summer holidays on the beach in Wexford, England.

As a young person, who did you look up to most?
My parents. And that hasn't changed.

What was your favorite thing about school?
The fact that we got a half day on Wednesdays.

What were your hobbies as a kid? What are your hobbies now?
Mostly music. I played guitar and piano, and still do.

Did you play sports as a kid?
Yes, rugby. But very, very badly.

What was your first job, and what was your "worst" job?
My first job was as a waiter in a local café. My worst job was ripping the jackets off books so the jackets could be returned to the publishers and the books themselves could be pulped.

What book is on your nightstand now?
All My Puny Sorrows by Miriam Toews.

How did you celebrate publishing your first book?
I quit my job in England and returned home to Ireland.

Where do you write your books?
My favorite place to write is in my office at home in Dublin. But I can write anywhere, and do: airports, trains, planes, hotel rooms.

What challenges do you face in the writing process, and how do you overcome them?
The biggest challenge is the point where one novel is completed and you have to start all over again on the next one. It's exciting but it's such an arduous journey that it's always a little intimidating.

What is your favorite word?
Champagne.

SQUARE FISH

If you could live in any fictional world, what would it be?
Narnia, of course.

Who is your favorite fictional character?
Homer Wells in John Irving's *The Cider House Rules.*

What was your favorite book when you were a kid? Do you have a favorite book now?
Treasure Island by Robert Louis Stevenson was my favorite book as a kid. My favorite now is *The Go-Between* by L. P. Hartley.

If you could travel in time, where would you go and what would you do?
To about a thousand years in the future. The world seems to change now at such an astonishing rate that it would be interesting to see what the future holds.

What's the best advice you have ever received about writing?
Write every day. Even Christmas Day. And read more than you write.

What advice do you wish someone had given you when you were younger?
Dyed platinum-blond hair and green contact lenses are not a good look.

Do you ever get writer's block? What do you do to get back on track?
No, I don't allow myself that luxury.

What do you want readers to remember about your books?
I want them to have a strong emotional response to them. To feel moved.

What would you do if you ever stopped writing?
Decompose. As I'll only stop writing when I die.

If you were a superhero, what would your superpower be?
Invisibility would be good, I suppose. For all the wrong reasons.

Do you have any strange or funny habits? Did you when you were a kid?
All the cups have to face the same way in the cupboard. And the volume on the television has to be at an even number.

What do you consider to be your greatest accomplishment?
Writing my novel *The Absolutist*. And I think I've been a pretty good uncle.

What would your readers be most surprised to learn about you?
That I can play an excellent version of "Sacrifice" by Elton John on the piano.

SQUARE FISH

It's been four years since Alfie Summerfield last saw his father, who left to fight in World War I. Now he learns his father is in a local hospital being treated for shell shock. Alfie isn't sure what that is, but he is determined to rescue his father from this strange, unnerving place. . . .

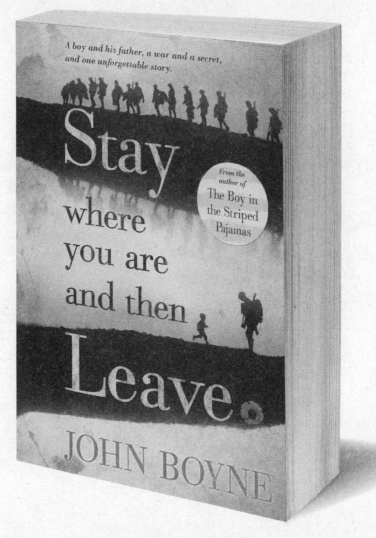

A boy and his father, a war and a secret, and one unforgettable story.

Stay
where
you are
and then
Leave.

From the author of *The Boy in the Striped Pajamas*

JOHN BOYNE

Keep reading for an excerpt.

CHAPTER

1

SEND ME AWAY WITH A SMILE

Every night before he went to sleep, Alfie Summerfield tried to remember how life had been before the war began. And with every passing day, it became harder and harder to keep the memories clear in his head.

The fighting had started on July 28, 1914. Others might not have remembered that date so easily, but Alfie would never forget it, for that was his birthday. He had turned five years old that day and his parents threw him a party to celebrate, but only a handful of people showed up: Granny Summerfield, who sat in the corner, weeping into her handkerchief and saying, "We're finished, we're all finished," over and over, until Alfie's mum said that if she couldn't get ahold of herself she would have to leave; Old Bill Hemperton, the Australian from next door, who was about a hundred years old and played a trick with his false teeth, sliding them in and out of his mouth using nothing but his tongue; Alfie's best friend, Kalena Janáček, who lived three doors down at number six, and her father, who ran the sweet shop on the corner and had the shiniest shoes in London. Alfie invited most of his friends from Damley Road, but that morning, one by one, their mothers knocked on the Summerfields' front door and said that little so-and-so wouldn't be able to come.

"It's not a day for a party, is it?" asked Mrs. Smythe from number nine, the mother of Henry Smythe, who sat in the seat in front of Alfie in school and made at least ten disgusting smells every day. "It's best if you just cancel it, dear."

"I'm not canceling anything," said Alfie's mother, Margie, throwing up her hands in frustration after the fifth parent had come to call. "If anything, we should be doing our best to have a good time today. And what am I to do with all this grub if no one shows up?"

Alfie followed her into the kitchen and looked at the table, where corned-beef sandwiches, stewed tripe, pickled eggs, cold tongue, and jellied eels were all laid out in a neat row, covered over with tea towels to keep them fresh.

"I can eat it," said Alfie, who liked to be helpful.

"Ha," said Margie. "I'm sure you can. You're a bottomless pit, Alfie Summerfield. I don't know where you put it all. Honest, I don't."

When Alfie's dad, Georgie, came home from work at lunchtime that day, he had a worried expression on his face. He didn't go out to the backyard to wash up like he usually did, even though he smelled a bit like milk and a bit like a horse. Instead, he stood in the front parlor reading a newspaper before folding it in half, hiding it under one of the sofa cushions, and coming into the kitchen.

"All right, Margie," he said, pecking his wife on the cheek.

"All right, Georgie."

"All right, Alfie," he said, tousling the boy's hair.

"All right, Dad."

"Happy birthday, son. What age are you now anyway, twenty-seven?"

"I'm *five*," said Alfie, who couldn't imagine what it would be like to be twenty-seven but felt very grown up to think that he was five at last.

"Five. I see," said Georgie, scratching his chin. "Seems like you've been around here a lot longer than that."

"Out! Out! Out!" shouted Margie, waving her hands to usher them back into the front parlor. Alfie's mum always said there was nothing that annoyed her more than having her two men under her feet when she was trying to cook. And so Georgie and Alfie did what they were told, playing a game of Snakes and Ladders at the table by the window as they waited for the party to begin.

"Dad," said Alfie.

"Yes, son?"

"How was Mr. Asquith today?"

"Much better."

"Did the vet take a look at him?"

"He did, yes. Whatever was wrong with him seems to have worked its way out of his system."

Mr. Asquith was Georgie's horse. Or rather he was the dairy's horse; the one who pulled Georgie's milk float every morning when he was delivering the milk. Alfie had named him the day he'd been assigned to Georgie a year before; he'd heard the name so often on the wireless radio that it seemed it could only belong to someone very important, and so he decided it was just right for a horse.

"Did you give him a pat for me, Dad?"

"I did, son," said Georgie.

Alfie smiled. He loved Mr. Asquith. He absolutely loved him.

"Dad," said Alfie a moment later.

"Yes, son?"

"Can I come to work with you tomorrow?"

Georgie shook his head. "Sorry, Alfie. You're still too young for the milk float. It's more dangerous than you realize."

"But you said that I could when I was older."

"And when you're older, you can."

"But I'm older now," said Alfie. "I could help all our neighbors when they come to fill their milk jugs at the float."

"It's more than my job's worth, Alfie."

"Well, I could keep Mr. Asquith company while you filled them yourself."

"Sorry, son," said Georgie. "But you're still not old enough."

Alfie sighed. There was nothing in the world he wanted more than to ride the milk float with his dad and help deliver the milk every morning, feeding lumps of sugar to Mr. Asquith between streets, even though it meant getting up in the middle of the night. The idea of being out in the streets and seeing the city when everyone else was still in bed sent a shiver down his spine. And being his dad's right-hand man? What could be better? He'd asked whether he could do it at least a thousand times, but every time he asked, the answer was always the same: *Not yet, Alfie, you're still too young.*

"Do you remember when you were five?" asked Alfie.

"I do, son. That was the year my old man died. That was a rough year."

"How did he die?"

"Down the mines."

Alfie thought about it. He knew only one person who had died. Kalena's mother, Mrs. Janáček, who had passed away from tuberculosis. Alfie could spell that word. *T-u-b-e-r-c-u-l-o-s-i-s.*

"What happened then?" he asked.

"When?"

"When your dad died."

Georgie thought about it for a moment and shrugged his shoulders. "Well, we moved to London, didn't we?" he said. "Your Granny Summerfield said there was nothing in Newcastle for us anymore. She said if we came here we could make a fresh start. She said I was the man of the house now." He threw a five and a six, landed on blue 37, and slid down a snake all the way to white 19. "Just my luck," he said.

"You'll be able to stay up late tonight, won't you?" Alfie asked, and his dad nodded.

"Just for you, I will," he said. "Since it's your birthday, I'll stay up till nine. How does that sound?"

Alfie smiled; Georgie never went to bed any later than seven o'clock at night because of his early starts. "I'm no good without my beauty sleep," he always said, which made Margie laugh, and then he would turn to Alfie and say, "Your mum only agreed to marry me on account of my good looks. But if I don't get a decent night's sleep I get dark bags under my eyes and my face grows white as a ghost and she'll run off with the postman."

"I ran off with a milkman, and much good it did

me," Margie always said in reply, but she didn't mean it, because then they'd look at each other and smile, and sometimes she would yawn and say that she fancied an early night too, and up they'd go to bed, which meant Alfie had to go to bed too and this proved one thing to him: that yawning was contagious.

Despite the disappointing turnout for his birthday party, Alfie tried not to mind too much. He knew that something was going on out there in the real world, something that all the adults were talking about, but it seemed boring and he wasn't really interested anyway. There'd been talk about it for months; the grown-ups were forever saying that something big was just around the corner, something that was going to affect them all. Sometimes Georgie would tell Margie that it was going to start any day now and they'd have to be ready for it, and sometimes, when she got upset, he said that she had nothing to worry about, that everything would turn out tickety-boo in the end, and that Europe was far too civilized to start a scrap that no one could possibly hope to win.

When the party started, everyone tried to be cheerful and pretend that it was a day just like any other. They played Hot Potato, where everyone sat in a circle and passed a hot potato to the next person and the first to drop it was out. (Kalena won that game.) Old Bill Hemperton set up a game of Penny Pitch in the front parlor, and Alfie came away three farthings the richer. Granny Summerfield handed everyone a clothes peg and placed an empty milk bottle on the floor. Whoever could drop the peg into the bottle from the highest was the winner. (Margie was twice as good as everyone else at this.) But soon the adults stopped talking to the children and huddled together in corners with glum expressions on their faces while Alfie and Kalena listened in to their conversations and tried to understand what they were talking about.

"You're better off signing up now before they call you," Old Bill Hemperton said. "It'll go easier on you in the end, you mark my words."

"Be quiet, you," snapped Granny Summerfield, who lived in the house opposite Old Bill at number eleven and had never got along with him because he played his gramophone every morning with the windows open. She was a short, round woman who always wore a hairnet and kept her sleeves rolled up as if she were just about to go to work. "Georgie's not signing up for anything."

"Might not have a choice, Mum," said Georgie, shaking his head.

"Shush—not in front of Alfie," said Margie, tugging on his arm.

"I'm just saying that this thing could run and run for years. I might have a better chance if I volunteer."

"No, it'll all be over by Christmas," said Mr. Janáček,

whose black leather shoes were so shiny that almost everyone had remarked upon them. "That's what everyone is saying."

"Shush—not in front of Alfie," said Margie again, raising her voice now.

"We're finished, we're all finished!" cried Granny Summerfield, taking her enormous handkerchief from her pocket and blowing her nose so loudly that Alfie burst out laughing. Margie didn't find it so funny, though; she started to cry and ran out of the room, and Georgie ran after her.

More than four years had passed since that day, but Alfie still thought about it all the time. He was nine years old now and hadn't had any birthday parties in the years in between. But when he was going to sleep at night, he did his best to put together all the things he could remember about his family before they'd changed, because if he remembered them the way they used to be, then there was always the chance that one day they could be that way again.